PURSUIT OF A WOMAN ON THE HINGE OF HISTORY

Other books by Hans Koning
(until 1972, writing under the name Hans Koningsberger):

FICTION

The Affair
An American Romance
A Walk with Love and Death
I Know What I'm Doing
The Revolutionary
Death of a Schoolboy
The Petersburg-Cannes Express
The Kleber Flight
DeWitt's War
America Made Me
Acts of Faith

NONFICTION

Love and Hate in China
Along the Roads of the New Russia
The Future of Che Guevara
The Almost World
A New Yorker in Egypt
Nineteen Sixty-Eight
Columbus: His Enterprise
The Conquest of America

PURSUIT OF A WOMAN ON THE HINGE OF HISTORY

a novel by

Hans Koning

Lumen Editions
a division of Brookline Books

ISBN 1-57129-045-1

Library of Congress Cataloging-In-Publication Data
Koning, Hans, 1921–
Pursuit of a woman on the hinge of history : a novel / by Hans Koning.
p. cm.
ISBN 1-57129-045-1 (pbk.)
I. Title.
PS3561.046P87 1997
813'.54--dc21 97-2550
CIP

Printed in Canada by Best Book Manufacturers, Louiseville, Québec.

10 9 8 7 6 5 4 3 2 1

Published by
Lumen Editions
Brookline Books
P.O. Box 1047
Cambridge, Massachusetts 02238
Order toll-free: 1-800-666-BOOK

κτῆμα ἐς αἰεί

I once stayed in an old Spanish hotel called Castel del Castro which means something like hilltop castle. It sat at the top of a street in a little town and from my room I looked down upon a road skirting the back of the building, and beyond it over the fields up to the horizon. In the early morning, school children and dogs traveled that road. After them it lay empty.

The thick-walled bedrooms were pleasant. The dining room was staffed by two students holding a part-time job, a young man and a girl who tended to get half the orders wrong. On my last evening there I walked out onto the terrace before either of them could trap me with the typed menu. I stood a while under the black sky with its blinding cloud of stars and then descended the hill, stumbling on the rough pavement until my eyes got help from the wisps of light sent out by the houses. At the bottom of the hill was a little restaurant, unrecognizable as such from the outside. It had a reputation, a star in the Michelin guide, I think. Enough anyway for me to have avoided it so far, as I was running out of money. When I entered its crowded room I saw that couples stood waiting for tables but the proprietress gave me a place for one at a little sidetable against the wall.

That day, at the precise moment of the shadow of a cloud crossing over the fields outside my window, a great feeling of unease had got hold of me, a feeling near to fear. It was familiar but I had managed to bury it for a time by running away, by traveling. In the restaurant, full of voices and candle flames, it became worse. Without success I tried to focus on the blurred names of the dishes. I extinguished the candle on my table with an unsteady hand. Lifting my head, I looked in the angry dark eyes of an old waitress. I looked away, and saw a young woman diagonally across from me, in the far corner of the room.

For a moment I thought she was watching me. She was not, she was staring ahead with unseeing eyes. Her companion was lighting a cigar and blue smoke touched her face. He was a youngish middle-aged man with the short beard French movie actors were sporting that year and he wore a heavy gold chain around his wrist. On his face was the frown with which the very rich give notice that they are on the alert against the envious world. In spite of these marks of power the man had no importance beside the woman. Once she had pushed her hair aside with an impatient gesture, I was overwhelmed, pained by her face.

This had nothing to do with "being interested in a woman." I certainly did not want her to notice me. When I ask myself now why no one else seemed to see anything out of the ordinary about her, the answer must be that perhaps they did, perhaps everyone was staring at her; I would not have known. Perhaps hers was a disguise, perhaps only a few really saw her. Not for a second did I assume she night be the wife or the lover of her companion with his cigar and gold chain.

I wasn't thinking all this in such charged words. I felt that her being there, extraordinary but quietly within the banal setting, lent peace, even sense, to things. I felt my unease dissolve, I felt a great relief. "I no longer think of death," Shelley wrote to Emilia Viviani.

I an not rambling. If the one Just Man may restore our hope for the world, then how much more may one woman do so, a woman beautiful not by the standards of men, even of poets, but by those of rivers, rain, nature? I am not, be assured, thinking of righteousness as male and beauty as female. To me, true justness is precisely female, not male. And there is a kind of female beauty which is its own and all else's justification, unquestionably because naturally. I do not bow to the Just Man or the twelve Just Men of an Old Testamental world.

I do not believe in that male world of Judaea and later of Rome. I believe how we, humanity, lost our way very long ago when we opted for Jewish righteousness and Roman armed pride. I am not raving; that much will become clear later.

In her present disguise, and the term imposes itself upon me, the woman got up and took a step away from her companion. She went ahead while he spoke through his cigar smoke to the proprietress. I think I heard him speak German. The woman used another door, she did not pass me. When he left, he passed my table and our eyes met.

I left too, to safeguard the relief I felt. I made a vague gesture to the waitress in leaving and then found myself standing under the stone portico of the house. Everything was ink black, I could not even distinguish the edge of the roofs against the sky. I heard echoes of footsteps but from both directions of the narrow street. Somewhere in the night she was walking beside that man. Then I heard a car start down the road where it widened into a square, a heavy machine. I saw the flash of white light and then of red as it drove off. That was the woman and the man, and their being in a car was better, her passivity in being driven more proper. I know it was one of the Mercedeses with German plates, those plates with the aggressive black and white lettering I had seen so many of in northern Spain. Not a white Mercedes; the man with the cigar would have a black one, a chauffeur waiting in it, reading a paper which before turning the key he very slowly folds—his one act of defiance. The man with the cigar might or might not be German but he worked from that narrow golden triangle, Zurich, Frankfurt, Milan. I knew that much instantly and without doubt. Now they both were sitting silently in the back behind an equally silent driver.

They are driven through the night. The French border guard at Hendaye salutes and waves the car through: this car out of all those passing he recognizes as the very Mercedes his father had told him about, a Mercedes in which a German general appeared at that border in the early summer of 1940 after the defeat of France, to give his instructions to the local police (the general had told the men to keep the frontier post closed to everybody; he had joked with them and then distributed Turkish cigarettes among them, tobacco of unknown fineness). The border guard's father had told him the story so often that he had begun to see it as if he himself had been there, as if he had been his father shaking hands with the general: the dust of that hot June month, the pleading and arguing of the refugees, the whining children, the rackety vehicles loaded with old mattresses and other junk, and then the gleaming Mercedes appearing from another, a stronger world of men without fears. It is now many years later, the border guard has held his father's job for a long time (the father is still alive, he has a little farm in the Dordogne), the shops of France as of Spain are crammed with every kind of cigarette and tobacco a man could wish for, but the Turkish cigarettes from that *General der Flieger* have never been equalled for him.

The man and the woman in the car are aware of the incident. How? The expression on the face of the guard, fleeting, white, in the arc light of the border post? His odd salute as if out of an old newsreel? Does the man with the golden chain actually murmur, *General der Flieger?* Unlikely. They had planned to spend the night in Biarritz, the rooms were reserved. But now he nods, although she has not stirred or spoken, and gives the chauffeur instructions to drive on. Intimacy, even the intimacy of undressing in adjacent rooms, has become unthinkable.

And by a far-flung coincidence or perhaps because it lies within the nature of things, the nature of a Mercedes automobile in this case, an analogous incident takes place many hours later at the next border, not long after Colmar. Here the car reminds the frontier guard (an old man, due for retirement in less than three weeks) of the selfsame automobile coming through in 1944, this time with two Gestapo officers in the back, between them the French ex-minister Georges Mandel (who is taken to Germany to be killed) sitting motionless, his face bloodstained.

This guard does not do any saluting, he waves the car through with a powerless gesture of resignation, then he draws himself up and shakes his fist after it. His two colleagues, playing bezique at the window of the guard house, see him do this and one of them remarks as he picks up his cards, "A good thing they're putting that old nut out to graze." The other card player does not answer, his thoughts are elsewhere.

Perhaps the woman in the car saw the old man shake his fist. From where she sits she looks into one of the big side mirrors and sees the world receding instead of the Mercedes advancing at its great speed. As they continue now on the German Autobahn, it seems cold to her after Spain although the temperature is comfortable for Central Europe at that time of year, sixty, sixteen degrees Celsius. While her companion smokes one thin cigar after another, she keeps stroking the leather of the seat beside her with tentative movements, not like someone appreciating the sensual feel of first-class leather but reluctantly, as if searching for but afraid to come upon the blood left after Mandel was dragged out, as if those stains could still be wet so much time, so many wars, later. But was it indeed Mandel, that prisoner driven into Germany? Or Simone Weil? Jean Jaurès? It makes no difference, him, her, then, now.

I am not much clearer about years than the old border guard, lucky old man about to retire into the perpetuity of a café table with its little piece of carpet to keep his playing cards dry. What I am clear about is that I must try to dispel her disguise, try to see her as she really is, away from the black Mercedes.

My eyes had adjusted to what little light there was in the street. I could now distinguish the stone reliefs in the wall across from the portico, a naked man with a halo, a saint, surrounded by small figures who appeared to be torturing him. The halo shone. The moon must be rising behind the houses, the air was becoming luminous. When I reentered the restaurant, I found it almost empty, with only a few men drinking together. The tired waitress cleaning up ignored me but the proprietress came over and said in English, "I thought we had lost you for good. We will bring you some menestra."

Later, when I was paying, she told me, "A reservation is always better. Here is our card. Tomorrow we will have a speciality, merluza."

"I'll be gone tomorrow. I have to get back to New York. I—"

She was not listening and I stopped myself.

I could ask her who that man had been. With his beard and gold chain she'd remember him. And I had seen him pull out a credit card. But what would I want with his name? "Good night," the proprietress said. The restaurant was dark, the waitress was holding the door impatiently. I walked back up the hill. The near-panic that had bedeviled me earlier did not return.

As on earlier mornings I was awakened by the roosters in the fields. I got up to look out, the fresh, early wind on my skin. The sun was rising behind a row of cypresses in the distance and threw a clear and glittering sequence of lines of light and tree shadows.

When you've been very sick, you're afraid in the morning to start finding out how you feel; thus I was afraid to start thinking or feeling. I tried to see my day ahead instead: drive the little rented car back to Bilbao, take a taxi or better a bus, wait in the row of cracked plastic seats at the airport beside the stands spilling their ashes. The green flickerings of departures and arrivals. On to Paris to get the connection home on the charter. Finding a phone at Kennedy (the relief of landing already forgotten), and then my apartment, cold or maybe hot and smelling of the scorched paint of the radiators, it fluctuates between one and the other.

I stood a while at my hotelroom window and finally I thought back to the evening before. It was indistinct now, a wordless image, but it was still there. She was still there. I went downstairs to tell them I'd like to stay another day or so. Yes, that was all right for the room but they had to warn me, there'd be a rock concert in the town square that evening and it would be hard to get any sleep. Local people had protested but the mayor was on the side of the tourist board. I thought about it but stuck with my plan.

Those newly gained hours went by quickly. Mist began to cover the bare earth and the grass. The light changed and drew away. One more turn of the wheel. When the church bells struck seven I went down the hill to the restaurant. Of course I was too early, the door was locked. This is Spain. I wandered up and down the street, not willing to continue to the center of town. I traced the outlines on the wall of the saint in his martyrdom. Then I heard the sound of a key turning behind me and a boy in an apron opened the restaurant door. I sat down at the same sidetable as the previous evening. It was very still in there, a soothing dusky light.

The proprietress came and lit the candle on my table although the last rays of the sun were just then reaching it. I shook my head to stop her but she did not notice. She did not respond to my little smile either which was to mean, "Here I am back after all. What do you think kept me?" She said, "Tonight we recommend the merluza."

"Ah, merluza! Listen, the man in the corner over there last night, wasn't he—I think I know him, but I can't get his name in my head."

"Merluza, in English, is what you call Hake," she answered.

"Ah, hake." I visualized a kind of big catfish, just the head, facing me from the table. "Hake."

We looked at each other. "The man in the corner," I said. "His name is on the tip of my tongue. I've got a terrible memory for names. I should have said hello. But maybe he'll be here again tonight."

"No. I think he's gone back home. I'm sure."

"Oh. Zurich, is it?"

She shrugged. "Binograd," she said. "His name. Excuse me," and she went away.

The fish was brought by the angry waitress although no one had asked me if I wanted it. It was just pieces in sauce anyway, no staring head. The proprietress didn't come near me after that. I could have sought her out of course but didn't. I didn't want to ask her more, I felt a fool. The hake was very expensive.

Later I sat down on my hotel terrace under a clear night sky. In the moonlight the paths through the garden were as white as during the day. I watched the two dining room students leading the hotel guests through all their badly typed courses. Then a howl pierced the night below us. Someone was testing the sound system of the rock band in the square right under me but invisible beneath the trees. I had forgotten about that.

The music started. After a couple of seconds it had become like a material presence solidifying the air. I hurried to my room where I closed the shutters and lay down with a pillow over my head. I even fell asleep for a while but when I woke up with a start, the music was louder still and I put my shoes back on and went down to the lobby. I had to find a spot at the other side of the building. They had a salon and when I had closed its double doors, it was almost quiet in there. Then I saw I wasn't alone, a woman with ash-blonde hair was seated at a piano. "Don't let me disturb you," I said and sat myself at a table covered with old magazines.

She played Lieder, in a high key, and every time she paused, the rock music could be heard. It was an electronics siege with she pouring Lieder over the attackers. I smiled at her but she quickly looked away and started playing again. I hated the idea that this pale creature would think I had tried to start something, and I turned my back and picked up a magazine. She stopped playing and I heard her close the piano. I waited for her to leave but instead she spoke to me. "Maria told me you know Mr. Vinograd," she said.

I looked. "Maria?"

She pointed with her thumb toward the curtained windows, toward the little restaurant, I guessed.

"Oh. That place down the hill."

"Yes, of course." She spoke English with an accent, French or Belgian perhaps, from the north. The muddy winter streets of Mons or Lille, pale girls going to school in their plastic boots to learn a foreign language.

As she was waiting for an answer, I repeated, "Mr. Vinograd. Yes."

"He's something else, isn't he? He has a villa in every city in the world."

I produced a smile slowly turning into a frown, admiration for Mr. Vinograd's real estate and horror at this excessiveness.

"Of course," she went on, "they're really business offices. Even in his bedrooms there is the computer."

"Ah, you've been in his bedrooms," I said, to my own dismay.

But she ignored this. She opened her bag which stood on the piano and after some rummaging pulled out a visiting card which she held out to me. "He gave me his card," she announced.

A young man came in, looked at us both and left again without closing the doors properly, and the rock music jumped the moat and filled the room.

3

Before dawn it started to rain. Lying in bed I listened to it and tried to make rain fit in with that chaste landscape. I went to watch at the window, a grey curtain of water moving across the fields, the yellowish road dark now with rivulets running on each side. Only then did I turn to look at the pale woman who was sleeping in my bed, her hair in the uncertain light hardly set off against the white pillow. I hadn't liked her the evening before and, equally debilitating, I surely had not liked myself, sitting in the music salon with a puffy face, dry throat, untied shoes. I guess I felt sorry for her when she produced that card of Mr. Vinograd so eagerly. This isn't meant in a patronizing way: she did not like me either. She made love impatiently and irritatedly, annoyed it seemed that my body wasn't just some kind of inanimate handle for her to move my sex in and out of her. It had been an escape from the all-pervading music. Now the soft rush of the rain was a marvelous sound, an enhanced stillness.

I studied her discontented face. The excitement and the consolation of a woman's body, of lying on a naked woman who is a complete stranger—it had not even been that. Maybe that is ruined too, I thought, lost by the modern fear that we are condemning ourselves to death right then and there. Perhaps we should now try again for a world of love poetry and serenades to virgins such as existed once. We have exalted our bodies too much. But then, what other link is there between people in our days? We won't be troubadours again, we will be lost in utter loneliness if we are afraid of those brief happinesses of chance.

"What time is it?" she asked. She was suddenly lying with her eyes wide open.

"Near eight. I didn't know whether to wake you or not. Do you have to rush off?" I hoped she'd say yes.

She set up, pulling the sheet up with her, and looked around the room. "I'd like to stay in bed," she said. "I have a dreadful room, right next to the kitchen."

"You could ask for this one, I have to leave this morning," I told her although I had decided in the night to stay at least one more day, to rehearse one more day the emotion of that evening. But I didn't want to share my room with her and I thought that was what she wanted.

"Please close the window. I'm cold. Do you want to, one more time?" She dropped the sheet but did not look at me but at her right hand, biting one nail and then another.

"I, I have a plane to catch. I'm booked on a charter from Paris to New York and also—"

"Say no more, Jack," she interrupted.

"You're not mad, are you?"

She had a little laugh. "You must think I am, what do you call it, very hard up."

At the Bilbao airport I telephoned my apartment in New York, collect, and listened with the operator to the melancholy rings. After one ring I already knew the apartment was empty; you can tell. I tried again from Paris without success. That was not the reason, though, why I did not go home on my charter.

Instead, after getting the schedule at the information desk, I took the airport bus into Paris, then the metro to the Gare de L'Est, and an evening train to Frankfurt.

It had said on that visiting card: O. Vinograd, Frankfurt a/M. Nothing else. That M stands for the city's river, I learned later.

I just made the train and found a seat in a hot second-class compartment. I put my bag at my feet and discovered a grease stain on my raincoat from the sandwich I had stuffed in the pocket as I was running down the station platform. "You'll like Germany," a woman sitting at the window suddenly said to me in English. "Everything *works* there. Where you from?" She had a soft southern voice and wore a rainhat. She gave me the smile of the brotherhood and sisterhood of American tourism. Do I look like a tourist?

A tunnel journey which leaves the openness of the ocean and penetrates into the dark heart of a continent of unvandalized telephones. Behind these looms its terrifying history, towns still burning, cobblestones still slippery with blood, ghettos still echoing the soldiers' "Schnell, schnell!" But the fields of America have been soaked in blood too, I said to myself. Still, I am now heading for an earth barely covering the furor teutonicus, the human fury, the human condition. That land is seeded with severed limbs, ashes of heretics, bloodless remnants of flayed rebels, rotting leather enclosing the bones it failed to shield, skulls choked off with piano wire. I felt my shirt stick to my back, the air was stifling. A young man appeared at the open door of the train compartment, pushing a trolley with drinks and snacks. He looked grim, he had a hard time getting past the suitcases and the passengers standing in the corridors. The train came into motion. I bought a black coffee from his trolley. My hands were shaking, I spilled on my bag and on someone's backpack on the floor.

Standing in a doorless telephone booth in the Frankfurt railroad station, I was peering at the directory entries in the dim light. The station hall lay lifeless at this deadly hour of five in the morning. A smell of water and of soot was in the air and a faraway clanking of metal as in prisons. Prison nights are part of my memory.

The directory listed three Vinograds. I held a handful of German coins obtained (after a bilingual argument) in the all-night drugstore where I had bought a candy bar for that purpose. Why I got them, I don't know; surely I wasn't going to phone the man at this hour? But he was not in the book anyway: one Vinograd was a hairdresser, one a kind of accountant (I have some German), and one, an O. Vinograd, showed no profession but lived Buttengasse 3A (II) which did not look like the address for one out of many villas.

Not a soul in sight. This city appears to have no homeless who'd look for the railroad station to spend a warm night. Or maybe the police keep them out. I picked up my bag and walked through a kind of arch into the square. Cones of light pierced the grey air, grey not like fog but as if the very air itself, the oxygen and nitrogen, were colored. The asphalt felt sticky. I'd better find a very cheap hotel. It should be one or two hours later here than in Paris—if not, I'd not find anything open. Or perhaps I would, near this big station. But there was no light in any building, no clocks, no lit shop windows, the streets abandoned, the houses low. It greatly surprised me, I had visualized the new Germany, the once West Germany, as filled with fluorescent lights and steel and glass, as in those spy movies where it provided the shock contrast with the dimness of East Berlin.

I know, there are two Frankfurts. For a moment I pondered the mad notion that I had come to the other one by mistake, the one at the Polish border. But I felt misplaced in time, not in space.

Once away from the station it was as dark as if there were a wartime blackout on. My socks were damp and my feet ached. When I came to a little park, I slumped down on a bench. The bench was dirty but I put my bag down by way of pillow and stretched out.

I fell asleep. When I opened my eyes again and looked upward, there was light in the sky. The stars had vanished. Above the houses straight ahead of me was a faint glow but not of dawn: it flickered reddishly.

I steered for it and when I had turned the corner I saw the glow was not of a fire but of a jumping name sign, the Frankfurt Carlton, reflecting against the steel sky. I hesitated, wiped my face and brushed off my coat. Then I noticed a large oil slick on the pavement mirroring the red letters of the hotel, and I rubbed a hand in it and touched my cheek. Really dirty, I'd be more convincing.

I leaned on the reception counter. Behind it a night clerk stood up and eyed me. "Car trouble, a breakdown," I said.

He liked that.

"And I was supposed to be in Strasbourg for a breakfast meeting. Give me a room please."

"What kind of car does the gentleman have?" the clerk asked with interest.

I could not think of a single car name. Mercedes. No. I just snorted.

"Ach ja," the man said and gave me a key.

My room was on a high floor where the carpet had made way for linoleum. I looked out over the eclipsed city and saw that it was still or again waiting for more bomber raids. I was tempted to keep my clothes on, to sit there in the security of being dressed, ready.

But then I dropped everything I wore, damp and sour from the fog and the night in the French train, on the floor and forced myself to stand naked and vulnerable at the window, I crept into bed, too tired to wash, defying the sirens and the church bells.

5

I slept very long, with dreams forgotten the moment I woke up. Dusk was approaching as I started pounding the streets of that town.

My watch had stopped. I wound it without setting it, I did not particularly want to live at the hour of Frankfurt. Phalanxes of men or of women, always the one or the other, three or four men with briefcases or then again a row of middle-aged women, flowed toward me and forced me to step in the gutter. Cars. Many bicycles too, unexpectedly, old and young people in windbreakers with advertisements printed on them or maybe political slogans; I couldn't make them out.

I was on an avenue whose narrow sidestreets were lined with bars. Signs in black, white, and red pierced the twilight. Groups of soldiers in harsh green uniforms were sauntering around.

And here women stood in the doorways, talking to the soldiers. Women with those same desperate and horrifying smiles, tight dresses, gleaming hair, that I remembered so well from our Vietnam television screens. The soldiers wore the near same uniforms but these women's faces were white and pink. Here stood the daughters and granddaughters of the women of Germany who had cheered themselves into a frenzy at the Sportspalast rallies for the Third Reich. Maybe some of them had even been there, they looked that old and tired. Maybe all those years in between had just washed over them as they unbuttoned and then later unzipped soldiers' trousers.

Neither they nor anyone else, whores, businessmen, shopping ladies, looked at me. They stared past me, away from me, through me. That must be because of my shabbiness. It was a miracle that the night clerk had let me into the hotel and I certainly couldn't go back there like this.

Here came a man's clothing store, credit card logos in the door which was propped open in spite of the cold and the wind. A cheap place where they wouldn't start telephoning to check on the credit card of an American. I went in and saw myself in a large triptych mirror, altar piece of martyred saint. Meandering around, I came to a rack with a sign saying, Reduktion, and it was easy to see why: the colors, blues, greys, and browns, were slightly wrong. They were all greenish. But there were also green suits, and with green, I decided, greenishness did not matter. Green is a good color for Germany, the color of forests and gamekeeper uniforms, nature and order. It would be popular. Fifty marks, you couldn't go wrong on that. The trousers were already finished off, the suit fitted nicely, schneidig, the salesman who had suddenly appeared at the curtain of the fitting booths said. That means, sharp. He didn't do any credit card checking. I resisted his suggestion to buy more. In my bag at the hotel were a clean sweater, and socks and other stuff.

That was a high point, I now see, when I came out of there in a never-worn suit, creased trousers, my first such purchase in a long while. A new leaf turned. I carried my raincoat over my arm, but it had suddenly become too dark to find out if I would get more recognition. I could test the suit by going into a restaurant, however. I opened a door here and there of places with steamed-over windows but withdrew from the smell of cabbage and lard and the faces coming up out of their plates to stare at me. I should eat in that cheap neighborhood; on the other hand there wasn't a chance I'd meet Vinograd that way.

I walked further and further, I came to streets now with cruising taxis, warmer street lights, an airline office, then a boutique with nothing in its window but a black silk scarf. It struck me how governments know to differentiate between their various citizens even with such things as street lights. Some citizens need neon fluorescence to be kept in check.

I passed a narrow, panelled door of beautifully grained wood and stopped. Here was a restaurant with an almost furtive name sign, the Hirsch something or other. The doorman looked past me but that did not count as a test for my suit. The Hirsch could not cater to people who hesitated before entering.

Now came block after lengthy block of apartment houses. Finally I had to turn in my tracks and go back, past that beautiful door once more which gave me hunger pains, and on toward the neon-lit streets with their peeling, mustard-colored walls and to the first cabbage place where I had looked in before. I put my raincoat on as I went in; I was too weary now to risk tests. I sat in a corner and fished the caraway seeds out of my food. It was not even very cheap and I realized my money was going fast. Walking back later I several times asked the way to the hotel but no one answered, they just hurried on. At last a driver at a stoplight pointed out the right direction for me.

Presently I recognized the streets, saw the hovering red light in the sky, and then the little park where I had slept on a bench the night of my arrival. There was a pressure of guests at the reception and the clerk gave me my key without looking at my green suit under my open raincoat.

Instead of quietly assessing what I was about on the thirteenth floor of a European hotel, I closed my mind to such thoughts, crawled back in bed, and started imagining the dinner one would eat in the Hirsch. But I fell asleep with the taste of larded cabbage in my mouth and woke up with it. Someone was knocking at my door and trying the doorknob, the cleaning woman presumably. I went to the window and was careful to look up at the sky only. A thin veil of cloud covered the sun and you could tell it was late morning.

I spent a lot of time on myself, I trimmed my hair with my nail scissors, shaved meticulously, put on my only shirt and tie. I knew what my priority was: before all else I had to go to that Hirsch and have lunch there, even if it meant fifty dollars out of the two hundred or so I had left. My new suit did not look quite as new anymore and it was very green in the strong daylight of that high floor. There was no help for that. I had recklessly asked the man in the store to throw away my old suit which he was eyeing with irony.

When I had found the Hirsch back it was past twelve. No circumspection this time, I sailed in and gave my raincoat folded to an attendant. The maitre d' hesitated one long second. But once I had been seated in the virtually empty place, my craving of the past eighteen hours had disappeared. It didn't even seem all that different there from the greasy spoon of the previous evening. My waiter approached, looking skeptical already, and I ordered venison to demonstrate that I belonged, that I was a hunter. He wasn't fooled, his facial expression didn't change. The meat came, colored rosy pink, and made me feel slightly sick.

The restaurant began to fill up now and a buzz of voices arose around me in various languages, the pitiless voices of gentlemen. It became warm, a lovely and different warmth from my train compartment warmth of two days earlier, the superior warmth of evaporating Eau de Vetyver and cigars—but to buy another half hour of that at the price of a Hirsch dessert did not seem worth it.

Back at the entrance door as I was waiting for my raincoat, two German marks clutched in my hand, he came in, the man of the gold chain, O. Vinograd. I was not even very surprised. He came in with another man who bore him a resemblance but more of profession than of kin. He still wore his beard but the chain had gone as I noted when he was getting out of his overcoat, which had a sable collar just like the one of Rod Steiger as the rich seducer in the Dr. Zhivago movie. The chain was too flashy for use on homeground, I realized. The attendant who had gone behind the scene to get my raincoat, perhaps to fish it back out of the garbage can, reappeared without it and completed taking off that sable-collared overcoat for the man. I saw now that he was wearing a black armband on his grey jacket such as Europeans do when in mourning. I tried to make myself inconspicuous by stepping behind a plaster bust, unnecessarily, for his eyes swept past me without focussing. He and his friend went into the dining room with the maitre d' and I held on to my two marks for the attendant who left once more for my raincoat.

When the maitre d' returned to the door I asked him quite casually if that hadn't been Herr Vinograd who had just gone in. He looked at me—finally someone looked really hard at me—he blinked (the green) and answered, "Yes, mein Herr." He then added sternly, "But Herr Vinograd is in mourning," maybe to discourage me from running back after him into the dining room for a stock market tip.

I stood outside that discreet wooden door—a sight which could never again make me hungry—and pondered all this. I had already found him. It was neither a miracle however nor even extraordinary luck. It was simply willed by me. Perhaps it was simply imagined by me. It gave me a feeling of control and of power. An autistic man must feel more powerful than Caesar or Napoleon. There was a whiff of fear in such an idea but I dismissed it. I am sane.

The cold wind had risen once more, the mistral of Frankfurt. To the left of the restaurant was a hackstand with taxis but there was no Mercedes in sight with waiting chauffeur. I decided to stay around until the man came out and to follow him, just to find out where he lived. Time passed quickly as I paced up and down, across the street, to stay warm and be outside the ken of the doorman. I did not analyze my intentions further. One move at a time.

When those two came back out, I recrossed the street. Vinograd was unhurried, he lit another of his cigars, shook hands with his companion, and got into a taxi. The companion took the next taxi in line. By then I was back at the hackstand and about to open the door of the third and last taxi when the doorman beckoned it and the driver jumped his car from standstill to the restaurant door, almost tearing my fingers off. With that one gone too, and Vinograd's cab vanishing into the distance, I stood there like an idiot, sucking my hand. "There'll be another one soon, gentleman," the doorman told me.

"Well, fuckit." And louder, "I meant to catch up with Herr Vinograd."

That surprised him visibly.

"Vinograd seems to be in mourning," I said after a pause.

"Mourning?" he asked. Or more likely, "Morning?"

"Ein Tod im Familie?" A death in the family.

"Ah yes. The wife."

"The wife? His wife?" I asked.

"Yes. Die junge Frau. Very sad."

I nodded at him and walked away. Maria, the Spanish restaurant proprietress, had said, "He has gone home," not, "They have gone home." Death had not been near the woman I had seen. She had not been his wife.

I could see the wife clearly whose death he witnessed with his black armband, still young, but sickly from her school days on. "She's not strong," had been the permanent phrase of grandmothers and aunts. But she was an only child, heiress from a local steel family which had reached its apogee of glory when they built a Big Bertha cannon whose shells killed men and horses in the outskirts of Paris during the long winter of 1914. The family had since been outpaced by Krupp and others and her marriage to the up and coming man with the beard had been welcomed.

Perhaps he had helped her on the way to her death, how many ways wouldn't there be for someone like him to get rid of an ailing wife! The price of his overcoat was sufficient to buy a doctor's fatal prescription. Perhaps he had felt that her existence crossed his plans, perhaps there was a link with the woman in Spain. Why had she been with him?

The sun broke through and I took off my raincoat and put it over my arm. My suit was still greener now, it had that shimmer you see on the bare earth when a new crop is about to sprout.

I asked the first passer-by where the public library was and this man even walked with me to make sure I took the proper turn. It was a big building and he was justly proud of it.

In the reference room I consulted the local business directory. It was a lengthy job for of course he came right at the end but there was nothing to it: the Vaduzer Investment Bank, with *Pres und V.*, O. Vinograd. I don't know what the V stands for. Only one telephone number. Hoffmeyer Square. I took a taxi.

It was a fanciful place, not looking like a bank but like a private mansion, with a modest golden nameplate exactly like the Hirsch restaurant. I only got as far as the hallway where a bemedalled veteran made me fill out a form. Purpose of visit: private. He left with my form through an airport-style security door and I waited on the stone bench which drained off the last warmth from my body. Eventually he returned and took me into an office where two women were answering telephones and typing on word processors. One of them told me in English, "Mr. Vinograd is not in Frankfurt."

"He isn't?" with a lot of irony to demonstrate that I knew better.

Her answer had just been a polite way of saying, buzz off. "It is better if you write," she said. "That is always better. You must ask for an appointment in writing."

"I don't live here."

"One should always write first. You may see the head bookkeeper, Frau Bartoldi."

"No, thank you. This is personal," I answered.

Her telephone rang. She looked from me to the veteran, waiting for me to leave before picking up the phone. The veteran made a half-turn previous to marching me out of there but I raised a finger and she did not insist but took her call. When she had finished, she turned to me with a loud sigh. "Yes?"

"I really—eh—" I was looking over her left shoulder at the back wall where a large photograph showed the bank building. On the top step, that very fat Bavarian politician whose name escapes me was seen, shaking hands with my man of the gold chain. Or perhaps not? The beard was there but he looked shorter and thinner.

"Is that the president?" I asked her. "Is that Herr Vinograd?"

The woman appeared surprised. She turned her head to look, then she frowned and said slowly, "Well, yes, of course." At that, my sense of purpose fled. Doubt settled on me and doubt became fear.

I saw now that I was making people uncomfortable in the same way that men carrying signs with prophecies or talking to themselves on buses instill discomfort. I suddenly understood how everyone had seen me, the Hirsch maitre d', the night clerk at the hotel, the librarian, these women: an odd individual speaking execrable German mixed with English, scruffy, caricature of the American tourist, harmless but a nuisance, visiting places and people he has no business visiting. They had seen no reason for my moves and now there was no reason for these moves to myself either.

I am entering an irrational world in which no one will follow me, where I will be truly lost. The unease haunting me is but a first stage. Madness will be the second stage.

The woman was still waiting for me to explain myself. "Yes, I'll write," I said and fled from there. The veteran had to hurry to the security gate to reach it before me.

On the barren hedge surrounding the bank one rose was left, half a rose, a few leaves and a bit of color. I picked it and put it in my lapel.

It was late afternoon and the light was the same as the previous day. But the city was deteriorating, I could see that clearly. Even during these last forty-eight hours the streets had become dirtier, the passers-by were bending over more deeply. Windows were cracked, alarm bells were ringing unheeded. Porno shops had black curtains in their windows as if they were undertakers, pharmacies displayed human livers for sale, artificial limbs. I took a taxi to the hotel, an interminable, convoluted, drive. Twice we crossed the river, the metallic sheen of the water covering unknown corruptions—the river *Main*. The second time we were on a bridge with high walls: I was not meant to see the water again but I raised myself from my seat. "You made a detour," I told the driver but he shrugged, pretending not to understand me. I asked the doorman to pay the cab. He started to explain that was against the rules but I did not stay to listen and rushed past him to the elevators.

I walked around in my room for a while to calm down. I pulled a chair over to the window and watched the city almost veiled in darkness now. I saw no light except the headlights of cars. The military blackout exercise was continuing.

Now was the moment to take stock. Hadn't I caved in too quickly? Reason, our present-day version of it, isn't necessarily the best yardstick. Animals flee unreasonably and hours later there is an earthquake. If my peace of mind or even sanity depend on my search, then it is rational in my life. There is no need for me to be afraid. Surely mad people themselves are never afraid of going mad.

I sat still and repeated those last words. I became aware of a hum, of the air conditioner or heating; under the sill a panel was visible. I tried to turn a knob but it came out of the wall.

I stood up and looked at myself in the mirror of the wardrobe. Now I liked my suit again. It had the color of ecology but also of its opposite, of uniforms, camouflage nets, jungle fighting.

Back at the window, I pulled the telephone over and asked for a collect call to New York, to the store where I work. I know the number by heart. The operator came back to say that they wouldn't accept the call and she sounded pleased with that, heaven knows why. I asked her to place the call directly.

Only after I had told them I was calling from Europe did they put the manager on. "I got salmonella poisoning," I told her. "I'm in Frankfurt. In hospital."

She seemed to be thinking a while. "How can I help?" she then asked.

"I won't be back in time. I need another ten days off, two weeks perhaps."

"Can you put the doctor on?" she asked.

I laughed in a sickly way. "You must be kidding. I'm on a ward, this phone is in the john."

"It must be unpaid sick leave," she said.

Early the following morning I took the streetcar to the old town. I had picked up a plan from the stand in the hotel but the receptionist who noticed my standing there with it, asked for the number of my credit card. He had forgotten to take it, he said. There'd be trouble with that when I got back. Stupid carelessness of mine. Never be conspicuous.

The streets were quiet, with few cars, some trucks passing us, and workmen on bicycles. We rode through neighborhoods where women were putting bedding out on the window sills and silent children set off for school. The hushed town reminded me of my childhood when my mother and I often went on long streetcar rides by way of Sunday outings. Those tramlines of my youth have vanished of course, our bus manufacturers killed them off. In Europe they still exist although I have since been assured that the streetcars of Frankfurt have gone too. But that cannot be, for I used them. I still have the white paper tickets with red numbers on them to prove it.

I got off when the car got crowded, bought an apple at a fruit stall and ate it while walking on. Mean streets with unknown languages on the shop windows, but here people looked at me and in a natural way.

I found myself in front of the railroad station or in any case, a railroad station. It was morning rush hour now and travelers were pouring out in streams. Different from my dead-of-night arrival but not happier. The commuters were grey-faced, extras in the old German movie *Metropolis*. I entered the station and saw on a departure board, in red, D-Zug, that is, express train, to Paris, 8:57 a.m. I could get that train and it would leave me with some money; the plane ticket to New York was in my wallet. My apartment, hot or cold. My girlfriend, my off or on or semi girlfriend.

I was standing in the hall with the impatient commuters streaming around me and felt like a child on the high board: to jump or not to jump. I wandered down a shopping mall. A travel bureau had a poster for a trip to a resort of the former East Germany, three days, all expenses taken care of, for only 143 marks. Photographs showed scenes from East Germany or perhaps of some other place, farmhouses and woods, forgotten paths, a nineteenth or even an eighteenth century landscape. Here was my escape and I had my hand against the door but went on. I ambled down a platform where two men were loading mail sacks onto a lorry from a train empty of passengers. They worked without speaking, angrily. When they had finished, they drove off at great speed, their lorry crushing my left foot. No, missing me by an inch. I shouted at them but they did not look back.

I sat down on a bench. The empty train pulled out and behind it another train became visible pulling out too. I was now looking straight into a first-class car, an old-fashioned one with compartments in green velvet, and at a window on the far side was she. I want to write just once, was She, with the capital S owed to the Greek goddess. In spite of looking at her across a moving train through a rain-streaked window, I was certain she was the woman from the little town in Spain. For one moment the railroad station lay in total silence. She may have turned her head in my direction. Then she was gone.

I was frozen but I forced myself onto my legs and ran to the other platform. I was too late: the letters of the departure board were flipping away and the sign turned white as I looked at it. I didn't consider then that I could find out what train left that platform at the time on the clock—8:50. The blank and hostile sign said, desist.

The name of the man who wrote the preceding pages is Lucas. He is out of touch with his time and with his place, his geographical home that is. His own mind has uprooted him, not war or persecution, which is why he cannot reverse the process and plant himself anew, as a refugee may hope to do. He is American in the oldest meaning of the word, forever waiting to move to a still different, still newer, world.

But he is in doubt about the real existence of this goal. His doubt is an indulgence, he has told himself that repeatedly. Steerage passengers taking ship in Liverpool had not afforded themselves the luxury of such thought, what mattered to them was to get away from famine, Czars and Kaisers. But how long does "getting away" hold good as a reason?

During the days of his last winter in New York (days had become lonelier than nights for him in that year) he had every chance to reflect on the ways we have available to continue shipping out, to save or more precisely *to spare* ourselves. He had come to think that he could do it if he gave up all thought or expectation about his country or the world, about anything but just himself. A more ambitious hope would make him a subversive in the literal sense, someone who rocks the boat and may capsize it.

He had done his thinking in a sea of time behind the counter of a Fifth Avenue book store. That store job was meant to be temporary; he was broke when he took it. But no better job had come his way, or possibly he wouldn't admit to himself that he did not want to change because its lack of demand made him feel safe.

He had been a reporter on a magazine and one day he would ("of course") get back to such work. If he was uncertain on that score he kept it hidden from himself. He was not even quite sure how his life as a journalist had come to a halt (when asked, he used to say, "I am an American dissident"). It had just happened, and he had not seen it as dropping out. He had felt he could not live anymore within those cascading and ricocheting certainties and doubts making up our world. I must step back, he had thought. If I can't go live at a Walden Pond, well, standing around among books isn't so very different. The day he had applied for the bookstore job, he had just seen a movie with Anthony Hopkins as a bookseller in London and the tranquil, learned atmosphere had made an impression on him. Selling books on Fifth Avenue turned out to be not quite like that. He stood around.

His first days he got into discussions. "You don't believe such stuff," he told a woman who had asked for *Assert Your Right to Be Happy;* he was hoping for a discussion which would help him through the long afternoon with the desolate rain darkening the avenue outside. "And why not?" she had asked. Lucas thought about that and said, "Happiness is not one of our rights." After a silent stare the woman had gone upstairs to the second floor and before closing the manager came down and told Lucas he'd be fired if he questioned a customer's choice again. He didn't, and they kept him on.

His university years had largely consisted of Latin and Greek and he did not regret them. He had never seen them as preparation for anything concrete. They made a world he could find himself in. He quoted bits of classical texts in his mind the way people mutter prayers or incantations. Repeating "Hepta epi Thebas" comforted him.

When his first bookstore vacation came up, five days, nine with the two weekends, he had signed on for a charter to the Castles of the Loire Valley—because it was the cheapest on the list at the travel agency. On the plane over they already passed pictures around of all those castles and thus he could walk off in an easy mind when they were standing outside the Paris air terminal waiting for their tour bus. It had been as cold there as in

New York. He had gone back into the terminal and got onto a plane to Bilbao in Spain, another charter, this one of Spanish tourists returning from a Paris visit. His neighbor showed him his purchases and told Lucas he had been lucky to be let on. It wasn't legal to hop a charter plane like that. I wish they'd arrest me in Bilbao and deport me back to New York, he had thought. He'd then be back there under an old and different flag, as of some great-grandfather of his from Ireland or Holland, a migrant.

Charters are our steerage travel, though faster. Looking back from where we are now, that may appear an immense advantage, but take the case of James Battersby from County Tyrone who shipped from Liverpool to New York in 1849. The voyage took five weeks. Think how the image "America" must have changed and evolved in his mind during each of those thirty-five days and nights. Battersby was a literate man. The letters he wrote to his wife in Ireland still exist. They make a how-to book, how to let an imaginary future supersede the fatality of the present. That was what Lucas really was after, but he had no chance to learn it on a jet plane.

10

The blank sign said, desist.

And yet, within a few days of that train pulling away from the Frankfurt station platform, I had an invitation in my pocket with his name, Vinograd, on it.

Coming out of the station that morning, I considered the day ahead and saw that I didn't have a notion of what to do with it, or for that matter with the days following. It was nine in the morning.

"Now do you know?" my mother once asked me; know the purpose of life, she meant. It was when I took philosophy at the university. She was kidding me, we didn't discuss such things. A maximum of pleasure, a minimum of pain? Not very inspiring. Now, this morning, I take my first step toward the purpose of my life. I conjured up the image of the leaving train. She is alone in the green velvet compartment, beside her a shoulder bag. The luggage racks are empty. I must wait; what other choice is there? I must wait for her return but not in my present anonymous state where if I fall into that Main River and drown, no one will ever know. I need a job, anyway, and I will take one where they don't bother with permits. I will take an illegal immigrant job even if it means washing dishes or carting garbage.

On the strength of that resolution I deserved one more good breakfast, and I went into a restaurant I had just walked by. But the place was too fanciful for that neighborhood, with waiters in tailcoats, tables with white tablecloths, and coffees served on little trays with glasses of water on the side. A European coffee house with instead of poets and revolutionaries, tourists with restless children and airport shopping bags. The menu was calligraphed on huge sheets of parchment. "Just a coffee," I asked.

When the waiter returned, he put a printed slip between my cup and my little glass of water which said, seven marks fifty. That is about four dollars. I thought I'd escape but he had not left, he was standing beside my chair. "Seven fifty!" I said.

"It's the minimum charge," he answered, looking over the glass curtains at the street outside, "until ten."

I was about to tell him I didn't have it, but as at the next table an elderly couple were observing my reactions with amused sympathy, I pulled out the money. "Those European prices," the man said after the waiter had gone. "They do take advantage." Both their faces had expressions of love for their fellow men and women. They were waiting for my reaction and expected it to be humorous.

"Nothing European about them," I half-muttered. "Try order a coffee in that place on Central Park South, that terrace." I was cursing myself, I should just have apologized to the waiter and left. False shame. There went my dinner.

The two were still looking at me, smiling because they hadn't understood my remark. "We had thought of going to Paris originally," the wife said, "but the French started that business of visas for Americans. And all our friends said, Germany is really cleaner, more hygienic. That's important for Fred."

Fred nodded. "But it's not as easy for us to find our way here," he told me. "My wife has French, you see."

"If I can be of service," I said. "I'm a licensed Frankfurt guide."

"You speak very good English."

"I'm from Vaduz. That is in Liechtenstein. We have the best tourism school in the world, we think. Tanner is my name."

They engaged me. I went to get a taxi and told the driver, "All churches, monuments, und so weiter," and off we were, me spouting names, emperors, bishops, wars, and Goethe who was born here, I think. They seemed to like it and then asked the driver to take them back to the Hilton where they were staying. They were tired. I was certain they were going to ask me in to have lunch with them but they didn't. Maybe they had caught me out in a wrong emperor.

He was the retired circulation manager of the *Akron Sentinel,* they had told me, and their neighbor across the street in Akron was the father of the Associated Press man in Frankfurt. He, the AP journalist that is, had picked them up the evening before and taken them for drinks in the club for the foreign press, very nice, the Ausland something or other, she had said. They gave me thirty marks which more than made up for the disastrous coffee.

I waited until they had gone up to their room and then got the precise name of that foreign press club from the reception desk, where they also explained to me how to get there. A very different neighborhood again, streets not poor but of a faded prosperity from a long ago past.

The Foreign Press Club had a porter in the lobby who took my raincoat and pointed me up a few steps toward a glass door without asking anything. Behind the door lay a vast, empty room full of easy chairs pointing every which way and tables with newspapers and magazines. An officious looking and nearly bald young man welcomed me (I was his only guest). He led me to a chair in front of a television set. "We better begin anyway," he said in English and turned on the set.

In front of a map of the world two newsmen were reading off a text. Presently they introduced a man sitting beside them, in dark suit, striped shirt, very familiar face. He started a speech and after a few words his voice was faded down and an English translation superimposed. The English was spoken in a tone of utter neutrality and behind it the German rose and fell through whole octaves. I tried to think of other things. Trains moving across the dark landscapes. A re-mystification of the world. A remythization. It could be possible. Why would there be no new quests for the holy grail, the golden fleece? Then the screen, blissfully, turned blank. "That was interesting," I said. "Controversial, of course."

The young man stood up. "I will now go and get you the transcript. You are with the—?"

"The *Paris Herald Tribune.* A special assignment."

He came back with a stack of xeroxed papers. "You feel it was controversial?" he asked with a look at the blank screen.

"In a proper way. Thought-provoking, I should have said."

"Your colleagues—" He looked around the empty room. "You will be attending the financial seminar next Monday? He will speak again."

"Certainly."

"I will get you a press kit then, and a badge. You are Mister—?"

"Rains. Like Claude Rains." I had been thinking of a film of his, *Crime Without Passion.* A man walks around with a briefcase containing the head of his victim. No, that sounds unlikely for Hollywood, but that is how I remember it.

Actually my name is Lucas. Like Luke the evangelist. I have always been happy with that name and that is my reason to keep it as new and unused as possible.

I accepted more papers and a glossy little book from him and a tag with a safety pin. He expected me to leave now but when I got up out of my chair my legs felt wobbly, I was so starved. Mistakenly I had associated the idea "Press Club" with "free buffet". "Do you have a cafeteria here?" I asked.

"Unfortunately not. However, there are some very first-class restaurants in the district. I will write down their names for you."

"No, please don't bother, I will find one."

"It is no bother. And we hope to see you here tonight, at six o'clock, sharp. The cocktail for the foreign journalists."

11

That evening in the press club Lucas was standing beside a trestle table with long rows of plastic cups, all of which a barman was filling with red wines and white wines although only a handful of journalists had shown up for the cocktail party. In the almost empty room the space around him was a void. His familiar panic reappeared. I'm far away, he thought. He stared at the rows of cups through half-closed eyes until they became reddish and yellow lines, wavering along the long table. Police barriers, ribbons around the scene of a crime. I had better get back to New York.

The journalists were talking among themselves in two small groups and when he traipsed past them with a cup of wine in his hand, no one paid attention to this man in the green suit which was already badly wrinkled. They're avoiding my eyes, the bastards. A schoolyard, old snow turned brown, Boston PS 198. The wall of turned backs, he standing by himself, looking away from the teachers who were perhaps pitying him. The relief when the bell rings. "You must make friends," his mother tells him that evening.

He returned to the table and took another cup of white wine and then a red. On his empty stomach they had their effect and he began to feel better.

A black man in a djelaba came up to the table. "Will you be going to the financial seminar?" Lucas asked him.

The man looked at him but did not answer.

"The seminar, next Monday?"

"That's what we are here for, no? That is why they feast us with wine, in paper cups." The man was about to turn away again.

"But this time they will just have to come to grips with a debt moratorium," words Lucas had overheard in passing one of the groups.

The black man put his cup down on the table. "Africa will come to grips all right, dear sir, and by not paying one sou more. My country which is Senegal has already repaid its debt twice over in interest. Now we say, to hell with the American Shylocks. When you prick us, do we not bleed?" He picked up his cup again, he had meant this as his exit line.

"But that is my line!" Lucas said. "If we are the Shylocks, as you say, it's us that do the bleeding. When pricked."

The man now looked at him. "You are an American?"

"You seem surprised."

The man laughed, a pleasant laugh. "I never met an American in such a suit. I would have guessed, let me see, an Albanian."

"You are perceptive. My father was an Albanian. He fled from Mussolini on the same ship as King Zog. He had been the court physician. I started medicine too but I had to drop out. I will go back to Albania one day now. In the meantime I write about finance to support myself." Lucas took a new cup of wine and the other man followed his example. "David Rains doesn't sound an Albanian name," he remarked, reading Lucas' name tag.

"I anglicized it, no one could pronounce it. It's Rreke, which means rainstorm in Albanian. The word has two diacritics. Maybe you can give me some pointers about the seminar."

"Such as what?"

"Who will be there? Will the big Frankfurt bankers be there?"

"They like to hear themselves talk, they like to sound like statesmen."

"You know of a banker called Vinograd, Dr Otto Vinograd?"

"But sure. I know them all. They like to talk to us, they like to explain to us indigenous populations how to do things."

Further questioning by Lucas showed that the African journalist didn't feel like discussing Vinograd or maybe he did not really know him. They drank more cups of wine together, though, sticking to a red-white-red sequence.

When Lucas woke up he found himself curled up in an overstuffed chair. The light was low, he was facing a set of dark-blue curtains on the back wall. He had become nauseous and the journalist had made him sit down in this chair. He wondered if he had made a fool of himself, falling asleep. His head ached. He closed his eyes again. I am no one, no one knows me. Even Claire doesn't give a goddamn. I've blown that too.

He scrambled to his feet but the trestle table was bare now and there was no one in the room.

Perhaps I am too hard on myself. I can waste my life as I choose. That's still too defensive, why pretend there are ways that aren't wasted? Our consciousness itself is wasted, we don't know what it's for. I mustn't fall asleep again.

His thoughts wandered. A sun-baked barren hillside, far below him the flickering Mediterranean. They were cleaning bits of marble, very carefully, he and a girl with red hair. Hyacinth hair. It was burning hot, cool in the shades of the columns. He could become an archaeologist, it is never too late.

The woman of the little Spanish town. Comillas. A previous perfection. I don't know what I mean with that. A perfection as from the past. Going back to our history from before the first battle, a feminine history. The battle was of the earth against the sky. The earth lost and that set us on our deadly course.

The steel of cars and tanks must rust and crumble and re-enter the earth as ore. Clothes unweave themselves and return to the skins of sheep. Tables and chairs fall apart and re-become trees. I read those words but I did not understand them, then. Whoever wrote them was trying to rewind history, to give us a second and last chance.

Lucas shook himself. He wanted to wash but every door he tried was locked. He shuffled toward the exit. The room where he had seen the porter take his coat was locked too.

He left the building and set out in the direction of the hotel. The air was very cold. Almost-senseless words marched through his head; he felt he was near some truth that would rearm him, but it remained: almost.

In the empty streets the stillness reigns of a city at its ebb tide. Seen from above, by his guardian angel or by a sniper on a roof, he makes an odd sight, a man in his thirties (or maybe forties, given that bald spot), a green suit whose shoulders, it now becomes clear, are far too wide and stick out like wings, his feet moving with a certain difficulty or perhaps hesitance as if he were walking through mud, shivering, an irresolution at the street corners and a generally strange combination of nervous alertness and lethargy—a pilgrim's progress but as of an Indian scout in the wilderness of cities.

12

Vinograd's name was not on the programs handed out the Monday morning of the seminar. I went in all the same. I had spent the weekend wandering the streets and reading tattered English whodunits sold for fifty pfennig at a bookstall I had come upon. I had been sitting with them on park benches, in an empty bandstand when it was raining, and once when the sun was out and it suddenly got quite warm, lying in the grass—until a park attendant showed up and told me it wasn't allowed. All this to stay away from the hotel during the day in hopes they'd forget about me and my expired credit card.

The seminar was in a modern university building and I was only too happy to get into a heated room, with the promise of clean toilets and with water coolers in the corridors. I'd go seek out the African journalist later. I fell asleep during the first session I attended, but only for a moment, and after that I kept awake by making notes or pretending to make notes. I didn't want to be questioned and thrown out.

When the lunch break came I hurried to the cafeteria in the basement. Food or better the lack of it was playing a large part then in my daily emotions. A line had already formed and it would take a while before I'd be close enough to the counter to read the prices. I promised myself not to spend more than two marks. I was inching forward, half-leaning against the wall, when a man came up, read my name tag, and said, "Mr. Rains.

I'm Alastair Baker. You think you could find time to do a translation job for us?"

Baker's banking firm was to present a paper on the last day and had synopses prepared in German and in English. Now they needed a French text too. I kept my place in line while he told me this and I saw that the cafeteria offered nothing for less than three marks fifty. "Why me?" I asked Baker.

"Every translation bureau in Frankfurt appears to be fully booked. And you were the only journalist there who took down the Michelet statement without putting on earphones. So I figured—"

"I see. I was just wondering, you took me by surprise."

"Your English sounds fine too," Baker said.

"I'm Swiss. I'm from Ascona."

"That explains it. The Swiss are great linguists."

"I'm the editor of the *Campana di Ticino.* Have you heard of it?"

"Yes, of course. A fine newspaper."

"Weekly."

"Weekly. That is what I meant. Look." He showed me the typewritten pages. The pay was standard, he said. I leafed through the pages while pushing my tray and recklessly putting dishes on it. I can read a Simenon novel but this was beyond me; there was the African journalist, though. He was francophone and he would help.

"All right," I said.

"Wednesday then," Baker replied, gave me his card, and walked off before I had had a chance to ask for an advance. "Nine marks eighty," the cashier at the check-out announced.

That afternoon I tiptoed in and out of every seminar without finding my African. Only when the day's session was over and people were leaving the building did I see, not him, but another African in an identical djelaba. And yes, he was from Senegal too and knew whom I meant. He told me I'd find my friend at the reception that evening for the undersecretary. "But there'll be a superfluity of security. Did you get an invitation?"

"No."

"Ah. In that case you must catch him going in or coming out. Do not bring a bomb."

"You are francophone too then, right?"

"Why do you ask that?"

I had thought I might as well ask this man to share my translation job but he looked at me with suspicion. "No reason," I said. "Thanks for your help."

I went half an hour early and waited in the street at the bottom of the steps of a Ministry of Finance building. Twice the police came to question my waiting there and to ask me not to block the access (which was about sixty feet wide). But then from one of the limos in line Alastair Baker emerged with similar dark-suited men and he said, sure, no problem, you can come in with my party. And the moment I entered the main reception room, I saw my African journalist drinking at the bar. He greeted me but none too warmly.

"I need your help." I showed him the Baker stuff and told him I couldn't do it alone.

"Why did you accept the job then?"

Perhaps we had not become friends over all those cups of wine after all. I am not a very good judge of people.

"Well, give it to me," he said. "One of our girls may want to do it, their pay is terrible."

I had planned to share the work and the fee of course, but I handed him the papers and turned to leave.

"Don't go yet, have a drink first," he said. He realized I was offended. "Did you see who is here? There, talking to the undersecretary. It did surprise me, no matter what I told you."

I peered around the room.

"No, there. The undersecretary is the little grey-haired man. Behind him. None other than your friend Monsieur Vinograd." And so it was; he knew him after all.

13

I did not really recognize Vinograd; this sudden confrontation confused me too much. But I recognized the black armband on the sleeve of his jacket, if not his beard.

The reception now became more like a press conference, with a lot of shouted questions. The undersecretary took the microphone and presently he introduced various people. The last of them was Vinograd who was thanked for something he had done with or to the Latin American debt. He took a little bow and turned to leave but was stopped by a query from a television reporter. All this was in German. After his answer there was a silence and people started drifting to the bar.

Before I knew what I was doing I had held up my hand. It or my green suit caught Vinograd's eye and he asked, "Ja, bitte?" Cameras and faces turned to me. I spoke, in English of course, the only words appearing in my blank mind: "Are we coming to grips with the problem of a debt moratorium, Dr. Vinograd, or aren't we?"

Impatient groans rose from the audience but Vinograd gave a surprisingly long answer which I didn't take in. After that, the retreat to the bar became a stampede.

A very young man in a striped ministerial suit had been going around discreetly with cards, invitations to a "closing banquet" for the seminar, as I found out when I got one. He had passed me by before but now he steered straight for me. Thus I became a guest of Otto Vinograd. His name was on the invitation as I saw when I had seated myself with it at a corner table to recover from my own rashness and to have a meal of peanuts and pretzels by way of dinner. The banquet was to be in his Schloss Vaduz, a castle that is. Clearly I had to take measures, the green suit wouldn't match the occasion. I must call Claire in New York, there was no one else, and beg her to wire me a loan.

And she did. Two days later American Express received two hundred dollars for me, enough to have a genuine haircut, to rent a tuxedo, to have some honest meals, and a taxi to the castle, with money left over for further developments. With her money came a message that she would have a week's vacation at the end of the month and planned to come to Europe. "See you," it ended. Here was an unexpected consequence of my telephone call, the more so as it had been brief and very cool on her side. She had cut short my explanations and thanks with, "Yes, it's okay, I'm sure you'll pay me back, 'bye."

The subject of Claire-and-me lacks luster. She is twenty-five, with a boyish figure. She is bright in a foxy way, knowing about people but not much interested in what I would consider the reality of one's life. She is fun to go out with but she looks at other men. I feel she resents me in a way. She once briefly campaigned for us to get married, but when I started liking the idea, she lost her enthusiasm for it. I guess our link is sex and that in spite of her aloofness; she is always willing but her interest in it (or so it seems to me) is that she considers it a kind of homage to her more than anything to do with love or even just pleasure. She enjoys the power she has over a man who is making love to her.

14

As a very young man Lucas had been briefly married. They had both thought of it as a great love. Now, more than ten years later, they still kept writing to each other and exchanging presents on occasion. Sometimes he felt as if they had decided to go through life separately but to find that love back at the end of it.

Claire had appeared two years ago. The first time she went with him to his one-room apartment and sat on his bed with her blouse off and her small breasts bare, he had been without any desire for her, and after a few awkward caresses had not tried to go on. She hadn't shown annoyance and called him again a week later.

The next time they were in his place, it was in the middle of the day. He had taken off his own clothes first, without asking anything. He wasn't excited about her body but about his own and he made wild love to her. Her flat belly now became a focus of an impersonal and soon obsessive desire to him. I wish I could rent it from her, what a pity that she is in charge of it, he once thought.

He also became obsessively jealous. She refused to answer his questions about herself and the evidence about her going to bed with others was almost—but never quite—conclusive. Perhaps she wanted other adventures, perhaps she was just trying to get even with him for his lack of interest in her as a person. He spied on her, he waited outside her apartment building to see how late she was coming home, and a number of times he opened her mailbox with a screwdriver after she had gone to work. He didn't particularly want to take her out or be with her anywhere else but in bed. Only when he was lying on top of that lean body of hers did he feel pacified.

Then her job sent her out of town for two months and suddenly it was over, so much so that he had literally managed to forget it. She reminded him once of his spying on her, and he indignantly denied it. That was after she had come back to New York. She became friendly, for she was sorry for him, first for his being out of work, then for being a clerk in a bookstore. It didn't humiliate him; she is not aware of the secret ideas of my existence, he told himself. They entered a calm take-it-or-leave-it relationship.

Things rarely take shape the way I visualize them. Vinograd's banquet turned out to be, us hoi polloi queuing for chicken curry while the VIP's were served first on a dais above us. The place was not really a Schloss either but a house, albeit a huge one.

As we were standing around in a kind of pavilion waiting and drinking sweetish champagne, me in my rented everything from silk socks to bow tie, an Australian reporter whose tuxedo fitted worse than mine (I had spent seventy dollars on the rental) said to me, "Quite a lay-out, this place. You've no idea how far back from the road it goes, this is just the visitors' bit. I drove all around it just now." It was the Frankfurt residence of Vinograd and his world headquarters, he told me.

When the waiters behind the serving tables were ready for us, I went to get my plate and sat down in the farthest row. The other chairs at my table remained empty. I could see neither Vinograd nor the African. Someone started a welcoming speech at the microphone with a joke about money being our object and our subject. I left the curried chicken and went out through the nearest door. In the corridor a waiter pointed me unasked to a toilet and from there I wandered away into the main body of the house.

Everywhere doors were not locked, lights were on. Large rooms followed one another, decorated in Versailles splendor and alternating with businesslike, Bauhaus-style offices. There wasn't a human being in sight.

From far off the sound of scattered applause penetrated to me.

I stopped thinking about what to say if I were intercepted. Calm came over me. I walked on, absorbing every aspect of my surroundings and wondering, has *she* been here? I scrutinized the little tables with china inlay, the spindly chairs, the vast paintings on walls and ceilings. On a dark wall I recognized the seduction scene from "Jerusalem Liberated" where the Christian knight is weaned away from battle by the Moslem princess or rather by his self-love, for he stares in a mirror she holds up for him instead of at her lovely round shoulders. Which is how the battle was lost by the Crusaders. How empty those words are, a lost battle, and how pregnant and bloody they sound at the time they are spoken or stammered by the living or dying combatants. The battles since the beginning of humanity's time on earth.

I looked at a Boulle desk with mother-of-pearl men hunting stags and wolves with bow and arrow. They wore rough beards and medieval skull caps; they looked medieval rabbis but I don't assume those hunted stags. In that same room was a large fireplace and its grate ended at each side in a bronze Greek warrior. On a table another long-lost battle order was laid out with soldiers and dragoons on war horses facing each other. After that came a hallway with vases from Persia and China on shelves along the walls, ending at a round table with a vase from Greece in red terracotta, a spotlight above it, on which naked banquet guests pursued a nymph, their bodies pointing at her with lust. A more genial banquet than ours.

In this silent, overly lit house, there was perversely an aura of loot about, loot such as war lords from Alexander to Napoleon to Goering have dragged with them from every point of the compass. It wouldn't have seemed out of place to me if I'd come upon soldiers, in any kind of uniform, sitting around that fireplace and breaking up the Louis Quinze and Louis Seize chairs to keep a nice fire going.

I came to a closed door. Behind it I found a bedroom, his bedroom for certain. A large bed with a blue satin quilt and on the mantel, folksy souvenir shells and a clock with a horrible china dog. One night table was empty, on the other was a book and a portrait in a wide silver frame with a black ribbon around it. Here was the Mrs. Vinograd for whom he wore his mourning band. A pale young woman with fear in her eyes. "To my beloved Otto" was written on it in English, but the ink looked fresh and hasty, the handwriting was of a man.

I picked up the book to see what Vinograd was reading and a folded newspaper clipping fell out of it and fluttered to the floor. It was a small photograph of the woman in Comillas. She looked straight out of the page but not at the camera. It had been the photograph of a group but he had cut off the others and also the caption. The date of the paper was in the corner above it and it was a month old; on the back was part of an article in German. He had had to cut her out of a newspaper in order to have a picture of her. The clipping had been unfolded and refolded so many times that it was wearing through. A corner fell off as I studied it. It dissolved into white and dark dots which with great exertion I could reassemble into a woman's face.

I now made the discovery for myself that this little square of newspaper was the only worn, used, touched, thing in all those rooms and that the paintings, hangings, furniture, vases, without exception were flawless. This house was not filled with a splendor as of the palace of Versailles. I have been in Versailles which is beautiful and old, beautiful by being old. Vinograd's palace was of no given time, it was a frozen time capsule suspended in space.

I could not stay there any longer. I took the newspaper clipping with me and I removed the portrait out of the silver frame. I shoved it under my evening shirt which had popped open at its middle mother-of-pearl button.

Going back I lost my way. I passed a room with nothing on its walls but a tapestry, huge and as of Bayeux but with twentieth century tanks and weapons instead of Norman ships and horses. I hurried on. A confused impression of history obliterated or rushed as by the fast-forward button on a tape recorder. When I came out into a corridor I heard music and steered for that, and only when I was in the last corridor leading to the dining pavilion was I suddenly challenged by an armed security guard who asked me in German where I had come from. I shrugged myself past him. I sat down at my still empty table, the plate of chicken still there. I drank the large glass of wine they had set beside it.

A chamber quartet was now playing and the VIP guests were descending from their dais and mixing with the others, going from table to table as if on a publicity visit to an old-age home. I felt they would not come to my table with its barrier of empty tables and chairs around it, and I picked up my glass which had been refilled and moved to a table nearer the front of the hall.

Four or five tables away I saw him, Vinograd. He and another man had sat down with the Japanese journalists I had seen at the Foreign Press Club and they were in a conversation with many smiles and nods. From them they moved to a table closer to me, then to one farther away. I watched their progress and felt the sweat run down my back. My neighbor at my new table spoke to me but I had no idea what he was saying. And just as I closed my eyes and said, you're a weakling, get away from here, I heard chairs scraping and saw Vinograd across the table from me.

A conversation in English began but I sat mutely looking at him. Fate had given me every help I could have asked for and here was the man, the only imaginable link with her. I became aware of the silence around me and looked up. Vinograd was staring at me and he bent forward to read my name tag. "Mr. Rains?" He was frowning now.

The others at the table were waiting for me to say something but when I didn't, Vinograd turned to my neighbor. "I understand you each feel yourself the representative of the public," he said to him in his staccato, unaccented, English, "but you must forgive me for remembering that the single owner of a publication outvotes a million readers." He smiled and there was a polite titter of response around the table.

I stopped looking at him, for every trait of his face was now engraved in my memory as was his every gesture, from the way he had blown out his cigar smoke the first evening to the way he kept his smile, contemptuous it seemed to me, while waiting for my neighbor's reply; the precise little movement of installing himself in the left back corner of a black Mercedes, the care with which he measured the drops of cyanide in his wife's tonic, his perusal of the tapestry of invasion. I saw that my table companions were again staring at me and I saw my own fingers, undoing the mother-of-pearl buttons in my hired evening shirt. He looked at them too, now. I put my hand in the shirt and brought out the photograph from his bedroom.

"One question, Dr. Vinograd," I said, putting the picture down on the table in the middle, halfway between him and me. "It is about her."

But then I could not continue. I stood up and made for that same exit door once more, avoiding everyone's eyes.

16

I got myself out of the Schloss and walked along a tree-lined avenue through fog and drizzle. Finally a passing taxi slowed down for me and that is how I got back to the hotel.

In the hotel lobby I had the surprise of seeing myself appear in the wall mirrors as the kind of well-dressed man who'd be smiled on by waiters and perhaps even by women. My mirror image assured me that I was not unhinged, that I had in a very shrewd way created a connection with *her*.

The notion of Vinograd having had a hand in his wife's death had come into focus as I was standing in his bedroom. The newspaper photograph, unfolded and folded so many times, and stuck in a book next to his dead wife's picture, showed that death as a threat to *her*. If that was true, my behavior had had the purpose of exposing Vinograd, if only to himself. He wouldn't think I was mad. He might well be afraid of me.

A feeling of self-satisfaction, unusual for me, came over me and affected me like a tonic; my body, forgotten except as a source of hunger, jumped to life and became aware of its frustration. I now imagined that a sense of strength emanated from me, while my tuxedo surely presented a striking contrast to the green suit. Nevertheless, none of the women who went through the Carlton revolving door looked at me twice, let alone smiled at me.

Finally I went up to bed, cold and hungry.

It was still dark when I was awakened by a knocking on my door. I looked out of my window at the erring lights of the town and saw a glimmer of dawn over the low building across the way. Then I opened my door on the chain and there stood a man who showed me a police card. I was to come to the station to answer a couple of questions. I put my evening clothes back on without washing or shaving and went downstairs with him. I never questioned him or protested. Without hesitation I had put on the tuxedo rather than my green suit: socialite arrested at hotel raid. I looked in vain for my raincoat until I remembered it was still at the foreign press place. The hotel lobby was empty.

In a small office at the police station, a uniformed man informed me that a complaint had been sworn against me on behalf of a Dr. Otto Vinograd of Schaffhausen, now resident of Frankfurt am Main. He said "a" as if he had never before heard of the man.

"What complaint?"

"Causing a Tumult," he answered, pronouncing it as a German word. "That is in legal English, an affray."

"He must be joking, nothing happened. Ask anyone at the table. My purpose was—"

The policeman interrupted. "We have statements from two eye witnesses," he said sadly. "It appears you threatened him."

"I confronted him, if you want, with a photograph. As a journalist I could have done it very much less discreetly."

"But you are not a journalist. And your name isn't Rains."

"It is my pen name."

He stood up. "Follow me please," he said. To my surprise he led me to a cell in the corridor and motioned me to enter.

"Wait one minute!" I cried. "Have you investigated the death of Dr. Vinograd's wife? Have you looked into that?"

"Just wait here," he said and left, closing the cell door.

I sat down on the stripped bunk bed and decided to give it half an hour.

After that I started banging on the door. The cell faced the entrance to the police station but I heard neither voices nor footsteps. I banged away until my hand began to hurt badly. Then I peed into the wash basin and lay down on the bunk bed.

I fell asleep; the day had had an early start. When I woke up, the daylight behind the little matted glass window seemed to be fading. I wasn't sure, though, my cell was too brightly lit by a wire-covered light bulb. My watch said ten but I had never reset it and I had lost track of the time differences. How had they even located me? Only the hotel had my name; no one knew me as Rains except the African journalist and the translation people.

I realized I had forgotten all about that translation, but Alastair Baker would hardly have denounced me to the police for that. I went to the basin and drank as much as I could, to quieten my stomach. The water tasted of iron and chalk.

17

When the same man who had come to his hotel opened his cell door, Lucas asked himself if he should complain about the arrest or just leave. But instead of setting him free, they took him to the courtyard where he had to climb into a police van. It wasn't the type seen in movies where prisoners face each other from benches, cracking jokes. This van had two rows of metal cells on a narrow aisle and they locked him in one not bigger than a large filing cabinet. The glassed window with little bars showed nothing but the brick wall of the police station. His watch had stopped. When the engine was started, he waited almost calmly for the exhaust fumes to fill his metal box.

Street lights and then long stretches of darkness awaited him. The fast, nauseous, turns, his stomach full of water, defeated him and to his horror he soiled himself. There came a stop at a country railroad crossing. In the still evening air the clanging of the warning bell carried across the fields. A middle-aged couple and a young woman were standing in the road beside the van, talking. They saw his face behind one of the little windows in the van and they watched him pointing at his mouth, visibly shouting words they could not understand through the thick glass and the clamor of the bell. They smiled uncertainly as if they thought he was acting out a joke. Possibly they assumed for a moment he was. Then, embarrassed, all three turned their heads away as if by command and resumed their conversation. Their voices became louder now, more German, punctuated by the bell, until the approaching train drowned them out completely.

When the van had driven on and all was quiet, the three suddenly fell silent too. The young woman muttered something about her housework and turned away after a sketchy wave of her hand. The couple walked on, the man shaking his head. The woman, certainly his wife, was about to ask why but then, deciding against that, yawned loudly. The man frowned at the uncouth sound. The scene lacked actuality, it was an episode from a documentary about wartime Resistance or the Holocaust.

The van's journey ended in the courtyard of a camp. As Lucas stumbled out, a row of guards looked at him, held their noses, and started to laugh with excessive heartiness. He was taken to an office where he was told they were holding him prior to deportation. "I want to see the American consul," he said without getting an answer. He thought they may not have heard the words but he could not raise his voice.

Back outside a guard gave him a blanket and a bucket, and pointed at a tap. "Waschen, waschen," he said, mimicking the movements of washing. Later they brought him to a barracks and when his eyes were used to the half-light he saw that it was packed. All bunks were occupied by two or even three men, staring at him, snoring, whispering to themselves, men coughing and spitting and incessantly clearing their throats.

Lucas was now locked within a pillar of lightheadedness, hunger, and the smell of his own feces. He convinced himself that he was not there. He was asleep in his hotel, imprisoned in a memory not from his own life but from the lives of others, possibly the memory of the twentieth century itself which has the camp at its core.

Perhaps it is a blood memory of the entire human race. But above all of the white race because with them it is *system*. Other races are as cruel but not as systematic. It is system which spells the distance separating the Thuggee stranglers of Bengal from the Germans running the gas chambers (or the Americans running Operation Phoenix in Vietnam).

Beyond a certain line, are there still degrees in cruelty? A hot and humid August, a Japanese battalion in northern China in the nineteen thirties. When this battalion catches young peasant women, they are stripped of their clothes and forced along naked on the day's march. In the evening any soldiers who want to, rape them. When the women are worn out, they are shot and left by the roadside. They often last for weeks. Husbands and brothers who try to come after them are buried alive, which excites some of the men in the battalion as much as the rapes. Is this more inhuman than the women and children waiting in the line for the gas chamber? Who is to know?

Inhuman! We must not use that word, he thought. What is human is poisoned. Only animals and young children are inhuman, that means, innocent.

Standing motionless inside the barracks door, Lucas had lost himself, had lost himself in images. No one stared at him. His surroundings were real. Most of the bunks were empty.

He got out of his filthy trousers, rolled them up, and put them in the bucket he had been given. Then he lay down on the bunk nearest him and pulled the blanket up over his face. It smelled of formaldehyde. He recognized the smell but could not think of the name.

A stone quarry. It was still dark when they were marched off. Lucas shuffled along, a chunk of the morning bread in the pocket of his jacket; the lesson he had once learned, to keep your physical dignity in adverse circumstances, never entered his mind. His self-discipline was gone. He scrambled up in the morning with a blank mind and crawled back unwashed into his bunk in the evening.

Perversely, for the first time on this journey of his, he was never hungry. He did not even eat his bread. He ignored his fellow men. Scarcely aware of the passage of the daylight hours, he did not try to work. When they had told him of the job he was supposed to do, he had not heard the words, and now he just stood in the cloud of dust which hung over the workplace. At midday a man came by with a canister of a kind of coffee or maybe it was soup and he drank his portion. It was lukewarm and thick as blood. Aware that perhaps it was blood, he vomited it up. Once, a guard approached him and he let himself fall to the ground, his knees pulled up in the foetal position. He had read that this offered protection when they kick you.

In the morning the old and sick stayed behind but when he returned at night he found them still alive, playing cards around the stove or lying on their bunks, smoking some kind of tobacco made from threaded newspaper from the outhouse possibly. He wondered then if he should stay behind too, but the prospect of being surrounded through the day by spitting, coughing, men was worse than the stagnant cloud of dust over the quarry.

He never broke through the surface and became certain where he was, but within his mind he reached a vantage point.

The images in his mind had led him wordlessly from this camp, back past the death camps, past the Chinese peasants buried alive, past the heretics at the stake, past the crucified prisoners of Alexander the Great. He had succeeded in bringing himself back to that first battle, the first battleground in our world, perhaps in the universe. Men had been fighting before; men and animals had killed each other for food. That was not: violence. At the first battle mankind had chosen a new path. Mankind was the proper word because the victors in that battle had been men only. Men seeing themselves as bright as the gods had identified with the sky and the void and defeated the female earth.

Measure had been abandoned in order to achieve this victory. Henceforth it had become possible for men to decide *to stop at nothing.*

19

A clear morning. We were summoned outside and stood in jagged lines while an official told us to listen for names to be called. But he seemed to have mislaid his file and a guard was seen trotting back to the office. Two swarthy men in Moslem skull caps stepped forward and one of them said in broken German that they needed a doctor. The official held up his hand and cried, "Warten, warten."

"Which means, wait," my neighbor in line said.

"What's going on?" I asked.

"We've got Turks here with radiation sickness. They'll be flown home, the Germans don't want them on their records here. No records, no law suits against the nuclear industry."

"What about you?"

"I'm an Irish refugee."

"Are you kidding?"

"No."

We stood and stood. Some of us sat down but the ground was muddy and slimy. The guard reappeared from the office with a bunch of papers and a few men started a mock applause. The official still didn't find what he was looking for. In my row a man pretended to faint and fell over. Or, he really fainted. A guard walked up to him, looked at him, and walked off.

"Let's help that guy," I told my neighbor.

"Don't. That one has got AIDS."

I bent over the man. His eyes were open and he slowly shook his head as he looked at me. Or maybe he just moved it from side to side.

The sun rose over the barracks roof. But it stayed visible for a moment only and then was blanketed by a dark cloud. End of that first clear morning. I felt exhausted now and turned around to go back to my bunk. No one paid any attention to me but I found the barracks door had been locked. I sat down on the step with my eyes closed. I was wearing the jacket of my tuxedo and had my blanket wrapped around me. My trousers were still wet: I kept washing them nightly, I think. Perhaps I had only arrived the night before.

I shuddered when I felt a hand on my arm. There was a soft laugh and I saw it was the African journalist who had sat down on the step beside me.

"But you are very nervous, my friend," he said.

"You! Am I glad to see you! I'm going out of my mind and I don't mean, in a manner of speaking. God, a familiar face. Are you real? Does this place exist?"

He shrugged. "Don't yell so. You'll make them itchy. What we see here is part of, how do we say it, part of the alert frontiers of democracy. In England two years ago they locked me up on an old dry-docked ferry boat. That was claustrophobic."

"But what happened to you? Why are you here?"

"You don't read the papers? Senegal's had a coup d'état, didn't you know? I thought I'd better request asylum immediately and by way of response they took me to this camp." He didn't seem curious about what had happened to me.

"I was put on an undesirable-aliens list," I told him. "I guess Vinograd did that. 'Unerwunst,' a fellow called me."

"That means undesirable all right. Vinograd, eh? What about the American consul?"

"Should I insist on seeing him?"

"No."

I did not ask why not. "Can't we just walk away from here? They don't seem very alert, that fence isn't very high."

"It may not be high but it carries a thousand volts, or watts, or whatever it is."

"Are you serious?"

He laughed. "How should I know? I just got here. The important thing is, we have seen those movies, we think it's a thousand volts. That's just as good."

"They wouldn't dare."

He gave me one of his stares. "You want to walk away? What about money? I had to hand in everything I carried."

"I didn't. Nothing. I was too smelly to get near to. There's something like fifty dollars in my pants."

"And where are your pants?"

"Back in there. Drying. But the door is locked."

He looked me up and down. "Let's go get them. Let's find a window at the back."

Half an hour later we were walking through a field of wild flowers and high grass with wooded hills along the horizon. No one had bothered or challenged us. "I still don't know your name," I said.

He stopped and held out his hand. "Lafont, Albert, at your service."

"My real name is Lucas."

"Is that a first name or a last name?"

"It depends."

"On your direction."

"Yes."

"But you are of Albanian descent," he said.

"No."

My trousers were damp and stuck to my legs. And the sun which had been out again, threw one last, sharp beam of rays across the field and vanished behind us. It started to rain. I was cold and every step was an effort.

"But we're going east!" I cried. "We're going further inland! What are you doing?"

"You don't want to walk all the way back to France, do you? We're almost out of this goddamn country, we're a couple of hours from the Czech border."

"How do you know?"

"How? But the cops told me. We took the train as far as Nuremberg. I informed them I always travel first class. They were very polite. They don't want to be racists."

We came to a road. "This is old concentration camp country," he said. "Now they use the camps, not the famous ones of course, for deportations. And for refugees."

"How do you know so much?"

"I'm from a very poor country, my friend. We do not spe-ci-a-lize" (he pronounced each syllable separately) "as much as you people. Before I was a foreign correspondent, I was our consul in Bonn. Of course that was for the old government. They had some good types in there, you know. Des braves types. I hope they weren't shot last Tuesday. In the coup, I mean."

He started to walk faster.

"Not so fast," I asked. "And won't the Czechs lock us up?"

That laugh of his. "You, maybe. Their own. Never black people."

I do not know when we crossed the border but it must have been long after dark. The rain never let up and I was shivering like a rat. When we saw a kind of police or army post with a Czech flag over it and a soldier outside, Albert said, "Let's just take you in there. You're sick."

I was, and they took me to a hospital in Teresin.

20

Afterward I was told it had been bacterial pneumonia. One day the fever was gone and the doctor who talked to me in a mixture of German and English said I could leave the next day. The hospital was free, he said, but they asked foreign visitors to make a donation.

My rented tuxedo, much the worse for wear, was now on a hanger beside the bed, and I had already discovered that my money was gone. My passport was still in the inside pocket where I had put it before going to the Vinograd banquet. I asked for my friend the journalist but no one knew of him. They had telephoned the American consulate in Prague about my case and the following morning a woman came to see me. I had just gotten dressed and was sitting next to my bed.

Our ward had two male nurses and she was the first woman I saw since my arrest; it gave me a sense of peace (no more than that). I looked at her silken legs, not slyly but with pleasure. Then my visitor opened her mouth and her metallic voice was at odds with her shiny legs. "I'm not the vice-consul," she informed me angrily. "I'm a consular assistant without rank." You could see she wouldn't let more than one tenth of what she thought escape from her. No words would escape through her teeth rows (Homer).

I told her my money had gone.

"We cannot be responsible for tourists who act foolishly. This is hardly the season for hiking through the Bohemian Mountains without equipment and in a—a party suit."

I tried to think of a joke but gave up.

She went on, "You were quite lucky. The authorities here are willing to accept that you crossed the border by mistake, in the rainstorm."

"But I'm not a tourist, you know. I escaped from a labor camp."

Now the neutral expression on her face finally changed. "You did? What was its name?"

"I don't know that it had a name."

"Here in the Czech Republic?"

"It was in Germany."

"Really, Mr. Lucas. Germany has no labor camps."

"Well, I was made to work. I was waiting to be—" I stopped. It would be stupid to use words like "deported" in front of a consular person. It must make them very hostile to hear words from that particular world.

"And how long were you in there?" she asked.

"I don't know. I don't know how long it was. The Bohemian Mountains, eh? What do you know."

"Well," she said. "If you want to file a complaint—We can take steps only with a sworn and notarized statement from you."

"You mean they have notary publics here with rubber stamps and where you pay fifty cents?"

She just stared at me.

"I've been in a state," I said. "Perhaps I better wait with any statements till I feel more clear-headed."

She studied her notes. "The hospital called us last week about you when they had found your passport. It says here you were brought in with a high fever, from a mountain hike with a friend. Where is he?"

"He had to go back to work. He's not an American anyway. I guess you're right, I must have gotten it all muddled. I was in a delirium, they told me."

She appeared satisfied that I wasn't going to try and make trouble, and pulled an envelope out of her bag. "We are entitled to offer you seventy-five Czech corunas."

"I don't smoke cigars. And anyway, the doctor told me I shouldn't—"

"Seventy-five Czech crowns as a one-time loan. That will buy you a train ticket to Prague tomorrow. At the embassy I will give you a voucher for a direct flight to the U.S. for tomorrow night. You will sign a binder to repay the ticket and the loan within three months, at fifteen percent per annum interest. We will have to mark your passport as valid for return to the U.S. only, until that is taken care of. The hospital will issue you a release and you can travel on that to Prague."

"Okay. Sure. Thank you."

"Please sign here, and here."

I asked, "How much is seventy-five Czech crowns?"

She frowned, "There are three tiers of exchange. It is enough for your ticket."

"Ah. You don't want me to get into any mischief. But I'd have liked to buy some souvenirs."

"Your attitude is somewhat surprising," she began, "considering—"

"Just joking. Just joking, miss."

The Bohemian mountains. That name had cheered me up considerably.

21

The streets of Teresin were very quiet. Every now and again an old truck with building material would roll by. Clearly the glamorous new age of the free market hadn't quite reached it yet.

I passed a grocer and a furniture shop and a closed little restaurant where a calendar in the window showed a blond girl in high heels pulling at her dog intent on chasing a cat.

At a corner I faced a half-ruined fortress. A monument had been erected in the square in front of it. It showed an elongated, thin, man shaking his iron fist at the sky and it was surrounded by a border of withered chrysanthemums. A sharp wind was blowing here.

The monument had plaques with inscriptions in different languages. I circled around it till I came to the English but then decided not to read it. I turned away and discovered a café across from there, with just two little tables and two garden chairs in front of it. I sat down and asked the man who came out for a coffee. He waited until I had tasted it. "Nice," I said. "Good," he answered.

"You know about that?" I asked, pointing at the monument and the ruins.

"Theresienstadt. Yes. This was Germany after 1938. Himmler, big concentration camp. Before, it was Austria, the Habsburgs. Was military prison." His finger traveled up the fortress tower. "Princip was in there, he died in there. You know of Princip?"

I nodded although I didn't remember, but I didn't want him to start explaining it. Later I remembered who he was: the student who shot the Archduke in Sarajevo, in 1914. Then, the Great War.

"Yes, Princip," he nodded. "Now all for, for nothing. You want more coffee?"

"Yes, please."

I was exhausted from my walk. The hospital orderly had sent me out after the midday meal: he said a walk in the town would give me my strength in my legs back. When the café owner had left me the second time, I put my feet up on the other chair. "That was no café terrace, that was our furniture, that was no lady..." Our pet joke. "Our" because once I did have a wife. The man I was then is a stranger now.

It was good resting there although the gusts of wind blew dust and sand in my face. I could make out some of the letters on the plaques from where I sat. They were of gilded bronze raised on a dark bronze background; the corner screws were iron and they were heavily rusted. They shouldn't have stinted on the screws. I was glad I had not read the multilingual message. So many muted outcries.

After a while I got up and slowly walked back along the tree-lined lane which led straight to the hospital. By then I had decided I wasn't going to any U.S. Embassy in Prague to fly home on their one-way ticket.

I had decided I had been lucky once more. A free rest cure. I was not going to give up now.

At the hospital office the next morning the orderly gave me a release form and told me to keep it in my passport because I had no visa. (He'd had an argument about this with a colleague of his who got furious and kept shaking his head.) Now it all became easier than I could have hoped.

I had a look at a map on the office wall and instead of catching a train to Prague I walked out to the highway going southeast, and I soon got a lift on a truck. After only an hour we came to a string of crossroads, part of the Prague circular system, the driver said. Lots of people were hitchhiking and trucks were stopping for them. One took me to Karlovy Vary which is less than an hour from the German border, and here the sixty-five crowns I had left after my coffees of the day before were enough for a ticket to Bayreuth in Germany. The Czechs stick out to the West in an unexpected way.

I got on a train filled to the brim with an old folks' outing and there was little hassle at the border control. Most of the journey I had been standing in the corridor and I got so worn out on my wobbly legs that I ended up sitting down on a newspaper, with people stepping over me. I showed my hospital release to the border policeman and complained in three languages that I had been very ill and needed a seat. He gestured that there was nothing he could do about that but then only glanced at the form and my passport and asked no questions.

In the early evening I stood in the central square of Bayreuth, an unlikely looking traveler in my battered tuxedo. But maybe that is the ideal costume for crossing European borders.

A web, a sea of street lights, flashed on. I had just one coin of half a crown in my pocket and looked at it a while, a little coin made of a dubious white alloy but with something friendly about it. There were a hundred times more lights and shops than in Teresin but there was nothing in Bayreuth the white coin would buy. Anyway, there wasn't anything here I needed. I still had half the bread the hospital had let me take along.

22

On my second entry into Frankfurt I was a lot more disheveled than on the first one. Hitchhiking from Bayreuth to Frankfurt was no joke: in West Germany drivers don't stop, at least not for someone my age. Can you blame them? My appearance spelled "unsuccessful" which is the western variation of being a dissident. Maybe I am making too much of it, but I spent many hours standing by the roadside while various drivers and even more their wives stared at me as if they couldn't imagine what I could be wanting. It was well past midnight when a nice couple driving a furniture van dropped me in the Frankfurt outskirts. A bad time to get to the hotel and try to retrieve my bag (if the police had left it there). I had to find a place where I'd be out of sight for the night. At least it wasn't cold and for once it wasn't raining.

I passed a long brick wall and came to a gate with a sign saying this was the town zoo. All lay dark behind it and it occurred to me that it would be a fine place to get some sleep. Maybe even some left-over food; I'm not proud. I looked up and down the street, saw no one, and climbed the gate with some trouble. I'm getting old. I was careful to stay under the trees and away from the few lights.

I've always wanted to visit a zoo alone without the crowds with their cameras and kids throwing popcorn at the polar bear. Here I was, wish come true. It made me forget how tired I was.

I sat down on the ground in front of a high-rising aviary. Well, high—not a bird's idea of high. They had owls in there, my favorite creatures, and also one small falcon-like bird. All these were sitting absolutely motionless. Birds sleep sitting on their entire bodies; try visualizing them curled up. It did not seem all that dark now anymore and I could see that some of them had their eyes open. Theirs was a new kind of time then. Time was standing still in the heads of these owls which is the same as saying that time did not exist for them. Time was and it was not. Here suddenly was a manifestation of that peace I have longed for but can never reach, just one endless moment of immortality without the fearfulness of "forever." Those owls were the luckiest creatures on earth.

I finally had to get up again because I had cramps everywhere and didn't want to fall asleep in the wet grass (the Czech doctor had warned me to take care). I went on and came to a cage with a species of small monkeys huddled in corners. They were asleep like people. But one of them was awake and moving very slowly through the plastic branches of an imitation tree. Here, and right beside the owls, was the opposite of their peace: a creature trapped within a hopelessly immovable weight, the weight of time.

I heard steps on the path and crouched behind the bushes. They passed and died away. I picked up a stone and started hammering at the padlock on the cage door. Yes, I know that monkeys can't fend for themselves at 45 degrees North but it didn't matter, I banged away at that lock. It suddenly broke, to my surprise, I hadn't expected it to, I guess I was really making a gesture. Now I pulled out the broken ring and left the cage door wide open. I hurried on. Maybe those notions about time and timelessness only show that my ideas were a bit out of control, what with pneumonia and a long day's journeying. Yet I remember them more clearly than the various *facts* of that period.

Eventually I came to a barn with an unlocked door and found it filled with bales of hay, a fine spot for sleeping. Every now and again mysterious sounds of animals had me come to the surface of consciousness. I wish I could have stayed in that barn for a long time.

It was nine in the morning when I approached the hotel. The timing was propitious: various tour buses were parked in front and there was great coming and going. But when I caught my reflection in the revolving door, I lost my nerve; unshaven, with bits of hay I had missed stuck to my evening trousers. I tried to go right out again but a man with two suitcases blocked the door and here I was in the lobby. Well, what the hell. Don't look in the mirrors. I went to the desk and caught the eye of one of the clerks. "I'm Mr. Lucas, I left a—"

"One moment, mein Herr," he said in an irritated voice and busied himself with someone's bill. Various people handed in keys. His phone was ringing.

"I say," I said like a character in an English play.

He turned, searched in the rack behind him, and gave me my old room key and a note. The note was from Claire; it was her handwriting on the envelope.

The room was as I had left it, with the musty smell of a long-locked place. "I'm in room 341," Claire's letter said. "It was too late last night and I was a wreck. Call me when you're awake." There was no date on the note. I put it back in the envelope and resealed the flap. I kicked off my shoes and stretched out on the bed.

23

Weary as I was, I could not get to sleep. I closed the thin curtains, took off my clothes, and searched my suitcase for my sleeping pills. I had to turn the case over on the floor to find them. I swallowed some and crawled back under the covers where to my own horror I started to cry. I saw the monument in Teresin with the faded chrysanthemums and wished I were still in the hospital ward instead of alone on this silent high floor. I wished I were a boy in my mother's house, the last place where I had ever cried.

When I woke up it was still daylight out. Claire's letter was on the night table. I had resealed it because I had planned that morning to leave it at the reception desk with the key as if I had never received it and indeed had never returned to the hotel. Now I opened the letter again and reread it. Of course I would go and see her, but not yet. No decisions before I found out the destination of the 8:50 train leaving from platform 7.

I washed and shaved in haste and put on the green suit. I rinsed the filthy evening shirt in the wash basin, at least four times, and hung it up in the window to dry. I found a couple of mark in the green jacket, enough for a streetcar ride to the railroad station. A streetcar, not a bus. I am sure.

The answer from the man in the railroad information booth was: *Strasbourg,* though not before I had thought up an explanation for him of why I had to know. The 8:50 was an express train with one stop, at Heidelberg. I sat down on the same bench where I had been the morning I saw her, and I concentrated on those two cities. Heidelberg was wrong, inappropriate. Strasbourg was another country, across the French border. There could be many explanations for her absence of luggage.

I went back to the information clerk to ask how far it was from Frankfurt to Strasbourg. He gave me a peculiar stare and then pretended to look through his tables, and out of the corner of my eye I saw several policemen closing in on us. They must have passed out photographs, he must have rung an alarm. But I ran right past them. Maybe they had come for someone else.

Back in my hotel room I got my stuff together. The evening shirt was nearly dry and I changed back into the tuxedo. Paradoxically, it made me less visible. I carefully got rid of every trace of my occupancy of that room, I locked the door from the outside and left the key in the lock. Then I went down to Claire. I didn't call first, I didn't see how I could make sense on the phone.

Thank heaven she was in her room. She looked pleased to see me. Surprised too, but that was because of my modish appearance.

24

Lucas was born in Boston in 1952 on November 11, once our Armistice Day. That date made him twin to the American hydrogen bomb, an idea put into his head by a classmate who was of the same age, one week older. When the Manhattan Project and the atom bombs were being discussed in high school this boy had turned to Lucas and said, "While you were secretly growing in your mother's belly, the hydrogen bomb was secretly growing in a New Mexico laboratory." "Well, the same for you then," Lucas answered but that hadn't helped. The remark had unnerved him. Although they had been good friends, Lucas never afterward exchanged more than a few words with the boy.

At seventeen, Lucas was in college studying for a classics major. The Vietnam war was midway but he might have had a draft deferment. As he had a flair for languages, the army also offered him an intelligence course with possibly a commission afterward. He refused both and two years later he ended up in prison, serving thirteen months of his sentence. He actually lost two years, for while awaiting trial he didn't do any work.

This happened before AIDS (which may now turn a week's jail into a death sentence) but even so he had been put in a state of apprehension by the stories of young men in prison divvied up among the old cons as prostitutes. His early weeks in prison were in a dormitory where they left him alone; he was thin but wiry and quite strong. Then he got a transfer to a cell with one other inmate. Lucas woke up the first night to find that man bending over him and saying something and he knocked him out with the enamel water jug he had taken into his bunk with him. The cellmate had to be taken to hospital. After that, Lucas was put in a cell by himself, in a storage room really, not more than twelve feet square, made out of a lost bit of space under the iron staircase. There were work programs at the prison but it was overcrowded and understaffed and he was never sent anywhere. Sometimes he was let out in the morning to sweep the hallway.

"Doing time" are words of precision. Kafka wrote that those of us who aim to live a long life should spend their days standing up in local stop trains. Prison beats that recipe, and the crawl of time was constantly at the surface of Lucas' mind. Unexpectedly, so was noise. He had had the idea, perhaps based on reading Nehru's memoirs written in a British Indian prison fortress, that he would spend his prison year writing a *J'Accuse* about the Vietnam war. His penitentiary wasn't an old Indian stone fortress though, but an American iron cage, clanging, vibrating and echoing, with sleeping men shouting and the water of the seatless toilet in his cell gurgling. Pandit Nehru would not have written his book in there.

When Lucas got out, he returned to college and to his classics. Some of his former friends were still around but they never asked him about his prison time and he never talked about it. He wasn't proud of his draft refusal; he felt there had been too much fear mixed in with his defiance. Not that he had expected to come under fire if he had opted for army intelligence, but he would have had to face an unknown that had petrified him. A police bus taking him to a federal penitentiary was security compared to that. He did himself an injustice here, because his main motivating force had still been without thought for his own fate.

He found out that he had been mutilated by prison even with no one ever laying a hand on him. He had faced aloneness and mortality in a way you are not meant to face them until your deathbed. Unease (that is how he labeled it) had permanently entered his life and if he had been able to afford it, he might have seen a psychiatrist. But he was pleased that lack of money made it pointless to consider that. Unease, anxiety, fear and grief, are part of the human condition, he told himself, and don't forget it. There is nothing abnormal about their presence.

25

Rain, dusk, car lights reflecting in the wet asphalt. It seems a miracle how the lights all glide past each other without colliding, more often than not, anyway (I once read in Thomas de Quincey of two coaches meeting and passing each other with a speed difference of twenty miles; the concept took De Quincey's breath away. Here the speed differences were a hundred miles an hour and more and the drivers were staring, yawning, smoking, talking into car phones). Our stage—Claire's and mine—was filled with lights moving and meeting at great speed and beyond them lay the dark houses and then the dark fields.

The sum total of the life of the town was its cars. Like parasites racing through the dead host body. I said to her, "Cars is where the light is. The city itself is under a veil every evening, they're having secret blackout exercises. That's what I assume."

Claire frowned. "Are you serious?"

"Sure."

She had been peering ahead but now she turned her eyes on me, to see if I were smiling. "What an odd man you are," was her conclusion.

It was the evening of that same day of my return to Frankfurt and we were on our way to Strasbourg together and in a car too.

It had been simple. Claire had had a bottle of Scotch in her room, she was pleased to see me and poured me an immediate drink with a "hair of the dog" comment (she chooses such expressions). She had asked few questions and virtually helped me in stitching a story together: with my hollow face and ruined tuxedo I had clearly come in from a booze-up. The idea amused her. She didn't seem interested in finding out why I had gone to Frankfurt of all places. Her European geography was hazy anyway.

I had been drinking her whiskey and wondering how to tell her that her loan to me had been used up and that I wasn't going to stay around for her week's vacation—for I had now committed myself into following the 8:50 train. I didn't mind hitchhiking without a penny in my pocket. Then I had thought it would be easier all around if I suggested she come along.

She was game, she said, for she wanted to see "a lot of Europe." I started muttering about her loan and trains in Europe being rather expensive when she interrupted. She had a rented car right in front of the hotel; she had come in the day before and if I hadn't shown up, she'd have driven herself to Paris next.

"What did they tell you about me at the reception?" I asked.

"Nothing, that there weren't any messages for me. Was there one? Hotels never get those things straight. They tried your room a couple of times but your key was on the board. I just knew you were on the town."

I wondered about the policeman who had come up in the night without saying anything to the hotel staff and I wondered about my bill. It was urgent to get away and to get away unseen. "I had already checked out," I told her, "and I had put my suitcase in the cloakroom. I wanted to save money. Who needs all these frills? It'd be nice to set off right away, wouldn't it?"

"All these frills?" She looked around her room (which was a lot nicer than mine; hadn't my trick with the oil slick worked?). "If you're talking about a good bed and lamps and big towels, I like them. I'm on my vacation."

My sudden hurry must sound odd. "Okay, let's try your bed," I said.

She was pensive afterward, weighing the outcome of a test? I'm on trial, I thought. But she began to laugh when, lying naked on top of the bedspread, she watched me get into my tuxedo. I laughed with her. "I was always meant to be part of the jet set," I told her.

"You look more like an out-of-work waiter."

"Well, let's hit the road."

"Okay then." She jumped up and studied herself in the mirrors. I was about to say something about how nice she looked but her facial expression stopped me; she was unaware of my presence.

I waited in the street while she settled her bill and off we were. She drove and it took an hour to get out of town in the rush-hour traffic. That was when I told her about the Frankfurt blackouts. We never located the Autobahn going south but eventually the city lay behind us and we were on a quiet two-lane highway. She said she preferred it. She put a hand on my knee and smiled at me. "It's an adventure," she said. She was very gentle now, friendly.

We bypassed some towns but when the next one came up, she followed the signs to the center and stopped in front of a hotel that was flying as many flags as the U.N. "I want dinner," she announced, "and I want to stay here overnight. I had a long day."

"So did I. But why this place?"

"It's good, they got five stars on their sign."

"They're not Michelin stars, they're homemade stars. Self-willed stars," I said.

"You're self-willed. Come on. It's okay." And when I still hesitated, she got out of the car and walked over to my window. "Coming?"

"I have a problem. I think this place—"

"It's my treat," she interrupted and walked into the hotel without looking around.

"I don't want it this way," I said when we sat at the bar. "But I haven't got a penny left, the last of my money, that's to say your money, is gone. Stolen."

"What had you planned to do then?"

"I didn't know yet. I still got my American Express card."

"Didn't they invalidate it?" she asked impatiently.

"Yes."

"For God's sake, Lucas, what are you going on about then."

"I'll pay you back," I told her. "You charge it, I'll pay you back before the bills come in. But we cannot stay in these fancy places."

"I'm not going to spend my week in your kind of dumps. You can pay me what you'd have spent yourself in your youth hostels or your Halfway Houses or wherever you go."

I decided I'd try to cash a check at the hotel with my lame credit card the next morning. With Claire standing beside me holding that Italian leather bag of hers and with her kind of clothes, it just might work.

26

Once we were in our room, the past forty-eight hours hit me and I dropped in my tracks, on the bed, that is. With a heroic exertion of willpower I managed to keep my eyes open and to make love again to Claire as she expected and then I more or less passed out.

When I woke up I saw on the luminous dial of her little travel clock that it was seven, morning, lines of daylight playing on the ceiling. Claire was fast asleep. I felt clearheaded and I carefully got up without waking her. We were on the second floor. I saw we looked out on a courtyard: a man in a cook's apron was putting out two garbage pails and then sat down on one of them and lit himself a cigarette. His apron was dirty, he was wearing sneakers with holes at the toes, but there was something so secure and confident in the way he sat there with his smoke that I felt a pang of envy. Envy of that man feeling at home sitting on his pail, me in this fancy nothing hotel room.

I picked up my clothes which were in a ball on the floor where I had dropped them, and put the tuxedo on a hanger. There was a piece of paper in the inside pocket. I had forgotten what it was and I pulled it out to look: Vinograd's newspaper clipping with her picture. I studied it near the window. I had thought of her in the black Mercedes, and now in Strasbourg perhaps, but never in a daily context with addresses, offices, names as part of her. I had not wondered about her name. The photograph could help, and with her name I might even ask Claire to phone Vinograd, pretend to be "an old friend from New York."

I made my little plan. I saw how opening my suitcase would probably awaken her: I put the tuxedo back on instead, took her car keys, and tiptoed out of the room. The hotel coffee shop was open and yes, they told me, there was a public library not very far off, and they explained to me how to drive there. I found it still closed of course but I waited, walking up and down a silent street under bare trees, feeling a mounting apprehension at the idea that I would soon read in a newspaper caption a name for her, at an ordinary, daily, function perhaps.

A woman in the library placed my clipping. It was from the *Rheinische Post,* she recognized the typography. She took me to the newspaper room and put a ledger of its past two months in front of me.

With the date in the corner of my bit of newsprint, I had the right issue and page. The complete photograph showed a group of men and women and the caption read, "Members of the Orchestra of the Chicago Opera which will perform at the opening of our rebuilt Kunsthaus." That was all.

Now I was happy it did not give her name. Telephoning Vinograd! For one second then I had an inkling of the emotion awaiting me one day at the end of the search; I could not define it. But it was not an emotion to be reached through banality, staged telephone calls. I cursed my own idiocy in that muted room with its little green-glassed lampshades. Then I scrutinized every issue that came after the one with the picture. Twice the orchestra was listed in the entertainment column and the last one said, "Final performance in Germany." There was nothing further about them but as I turned the pages, the name Vinograd leaped at me.

TRAGÖDIE, a one column item at the bottom of the front page. Herrn Doktor Otto Vinograd's wife had drowned. The Vinograds had been guests on the yacht of Tony Villanova, the Monegasque banker. The accident had occurred at the beach of Comillas, on the north shore of Spain.

A few days after this Tragödie, he had been blowing out his cigar smoke in the Comillas restaurant.

Back at the hotel I found Claire in the coffeeshop with her travel bag at her feet. "I'm so glad you conquered all those qualms you had yesterday," she said, "enough anyway to steal my car."

"I didn't want to wake you! I was sure I'd be back before you opened your eyes. Did you have breakfast yet?"

"Two breakfasts. I also counted the shepherds on the wallpaper here twice. Can we get this show on the road, as you call it?"

"Just let me go cash a check at the reception," I said.

"How are you going to do that?"

"Well, it would help if you came with me and stood next to me."

She looked me up and down and began to smile, though not at me. "Give me the keys," she said, "I'd rather wait for you in the car."

Without her and Gucci, my check did not make it.

The road we were on led through the heart of town and I passed the library street again. "That's where I was this morning," I began. I was going to try and tell her my tale now, but she did not react to those words and did not take her eyes off the road.

I didn't say anything more.

"You are a funny man," she told me after a long silence. "How did you figure that that retired army major at the desk was ever going to cash a check for you? You're not even shaven! I'm sure he would have liked to give you ten days light arrest for that. You've got ketchup on your collar. That tuxedo begins to look like a joke. Aren't you getting tired of your drop-out act? I am."

"I can't have ketchup on my collar, I never use it. It must be blood."

27

Otto Vinograd and his wife had tea with their breakfasts. "Wie Engländer," like the English, their host Tony Villanova said and that remark amused everyone although it is not clear why.

"I'll only have toast," Inge said, "for I'm going for a swim afterward." She was already in her bathing suit, an old-fashioned one-piece with wide shoulderstraps. Her arms and legs looked pale in the sunlight reflected on the dark water. They were thin. How unsensual her body has always been, Vinograd thought. Once they used to tell me how pretty she was. Did they mean it or were they making a fool of me? Freckled shoulders, her collarbones stretching the skin, the blue suit with its border of little white fishes. He felt sorry for her. Poor devil. She caught his look and he gave her a smile she did not return. He half-closed his eyes and the border of white fishes looked like a ticker-tape. "You've got goose bumps," he said.

"The air is cold this morning. But the water will warm me."

I must say something friendly. "I'll row you to the point. The water in the bay looks dirty today."

"You city people." Villanova shook his head. "The water is fine. That's mud from the tide. Absolutely natural. But I'll call the motorboat out for you if you want, Inge."

"I don't mind mud. I'm not city people. I'm a farm girl."

"Your natural mud smells like my chemical plant in Schaffhausen,"

Vinograd told him. "I like the rowing, I need the exercise. I do nothing here all day."

Vinograd rowed his wife to the rocky promontory of Comillas. High above them they saw the restaurant where they had all dined the night before, its shutters now closed. Inge felt a moment's nausea. The black lobster they had shown her, alive first and then red, boiled to death in sea water. She shivered and Vinograd frowned. "I'm fine," she said. She stepped from the rowboat onto a rock and dived in, an elegant dive. The sea water was cold but then pleasantly warm, then, not quite believably, it became too warm, hot, torturous, shattering nerves and veins. How long could a carapace shield one and keep one alive, seconds, minutes? The silent scream, impossible to imagine.

Vinograd opened a newspaper. The current was out and the boat, tied to a boulder, danced lightly on the water and pointed itself steadily toward the horizon. There was no need to work on keeping it away from the rocks.

After he had plowed his way through the newspapers which he did at great speed, Vinograd looked around. Inge was not drying herself on the rocks, her straps rolled down just a few inches, as was her habit. He loosened the rope and rowed a half circle, scanning the rocks and the sea. "She has swum back to the yacht, she likes to swim to a fixed point at some distance," he said aloud.

Rowing himself back, Vinograd encountered a little local outboard. Its skipper wore a duffel jacket and a sailor's cap, but whether he was a man whose profession is with the sea or a tourist who had profited from the fall sale at the local marine store was uncertain. A white speck at the back of his sailor's cap could be a piece of the torn-off price tag, or it could be something different, a gull's droppings. From where Vinograd passed him, some twenty feet away, it was impossible to tell. As their eyes met, the outboard skipper gave Vinograd a smart imitation-navy salute, and Vinograd started to lift his hand in response but checked himself just in time.

Her aloof profile. Yes, Claire, I know I am just a store clerk, but you might say I'm under cover, like a secret emissary. I am on a search. You will see. Or maybe you will not.

We surround ourselves with goodies to keep us going but the world's treasures and resources were hardly created to provide us with pacifiers. Have you ever considered that, Claire. Perhaps we are just parasites in the universe.

"Why do you have to be different?" she asked but not as if she expected an answer.

I damn well hope so. I aspire to be—no phony modesty now—I aspire to be a hero for our time, to break away from the old heroism of anger that has poisoned us. And, if you want to hear this, that is the reason I am sitting in your car. Not for a vacation, not to see "a lot of Europe."

I am on a search, trying to find a woman. Indeed, a beautiful woman, but such words would give you a false connotation. It's not about someone with a beautiful face or a beautiful body, it is about a prophetic beauty, but prophetic of the past, the past of the earth which was female or feminine. But if I would say all this aloud, Claire would stop the car and ask me to get out. She would have thought I was going mad. I am not, though.

We drove the rest of the way in silence. Stretches of wood were followed by factories and industrial slums. Every now and again a glimpse of the Rhine was visible. It looked cool and pure in its grey-blueness even though it is a sewer. Then we passed signs announcing the approach of the border and France, "three kilometers," "one kilometer." Without saying or asking anything, she was driving us to Strasbourg.

And here was the line for the customs post at Kehl where the Rhine bridge crosses. Comb hair, dust off jacket. Most cars hardly stopped but the border guard stood a while with my passport in his hand, studying me through the open car window. I plead guilty to my appearance. Then he waved us on without a word. As we drove over the bridge, I saw myself get out and sit down on that no man's, everyman's, stretch of asphalt. Or even better, on the little island below us in the river, just an overgrown rock with some trees and an open space in the middle. You could build a hut there, you'd row to France in the night for bread and wine, and to Germany to steal some money. Not in anger, not like Achilles in his tent, not dropping out, but to think, to rethink a history for us without the traces of running blood woven through its fabric.

The café terrace under a red brick arcade had a view of Strasbourg cathedral or to be precise, of the large white blocks making up one corner. Alone on the terrace, I kept picking up my tiny cup of coffee for the last few sips but putting it down with the coffee untouched, lest the waiter would come and take it away.

Claire had dropped me off as we entered the town; she was going to find a hotel for us but by herself. She didn't want to travel "like a couple which we aren't," she said, she wanted to do things on her own now, her first time abroad. "Besides, the way you look, they'd say they had no room."

"They'd say it in French if at all and you wouldn't understand."

"I'll understand whatever gives, don't you worry. I'll come for you afterward. Maybe."

I could have been more gracious about it, it was natural that she wanted to be adventurous. I'd apologize. I hate possessiveness.

The street lay virtually empty of life in front of me. At the far end a man stood leaning against the railing of the cathedral, reading a newspaper. Or pretending to, like a character in a detective story. An old woman with a dog took her endless time getting by the café terrace. I had expected it to be all different here from Frankfurt and in its own way it was as somber. There were store windows, brightly lit this rainy early afternoon. The stores offered beds, washing machines, carpets, they were large places and devoid of any human being going in or out. The white corner stones of the cathedral reflected blue in the bluish light of the shop across from it, a pharmacy perhaps. Above the roofs the sky, reddish-grey, was cut up by clumps of TV aerials about to crush into the streets. I tilted my chair up against the table and entered the café.

The waiter who had been leaning against the bar took a step toward me but I ignored him and rushed down the stairs, where the directory in the basement phone booth listed an "Orchestre National" in Strasbourg and nothing else under the heading "Musique" in the business pages. The toilet mirror gave me a pleasant surprise. Claire is wrong. I and my tuxedo haven't become shabbier on my journey but, more artistic. I don't look like an out of work waiter anymore.

Back out on the terrace I found my chair had been put upright and my only half-empty cup taken away. I kept going and once around the corner started running. They put you in jail in France for not paying your coffee if you're a foreigner, or so I've always been told.

More people and cars filled the streets here, this was the old town. An English-speaking policeman pointed out the concert hall and it was at the address I had written down for the national orchestra. I circled the dark building and came at the back to lit windows with desks under fluorescent lights. I decided to go in, a violinist who has to get in touch with the Chicago Opera Orchestra. Were they in town?

They had been, but they had gone. Where? The woman, young, in a long black dress, did not know. "I heard them," she said in English, "They were quite good." She was turning away but I took out my newspaper clipping.

"Did you see her, do you remember?" I asked. She looked and the other woman came forward to look too. They smiled at me. No, they didn't remember. They had been quite high up in the hall.

The girl in the black dress picked up the phone and got into an animated conversation; the other one went back to her work. I frowned at the one chatting on the phone. "C'est très important," I said. It was, it was crucial; if I failed to get it, fate, chance, whatever had led me so far, had run its course. She covered her phone with one hand. "They have gone to Paris," she said. "They are always, I mean they are *still* there. At the Salle Martel. Martel. I will write it down."

When I came out, it had started raining again. I tilted my head upward to wash all tears away, I started singing, "Salle Martel, Salle Martel." Two children stared at me, burst into giggles, and ran narrowly past me.

30

Back at the arcade I found the café terrace still empty. I couldn't go look inside because I didn't have the money for my coffee. Perhaps Claire had come and gone.

Before, I had avoided really looking at the cathedral; now it was all different and easier. I got as close as possible and stared straight up along the wall. They had put half-spheres of metal on it like the dots at the end of a puzzled sentence and these led the eye up to the spire and then down to a circular window that portrayed the Last Judgment. I thought here were metaphysical architectonics but then saw they were burglar alarms, and remarkably many of them. Perpendicular below the window stood Claire's car. It was unlocked and I installed myself on the rear seat and took my leaking shoes off.

For a short moment the rain came down so hard that the street, the houses, and the walls of the church vanished. The rain was hammering on the metal roof with curtains of water around me and nothing else. I was on a high plateau in a landscape empty of human life. The rain stopped.

Claire appeared carrying packages, looking happy and very young.

"Strasboúrg agrees with me," she said. She had taken to pronouncing the name the French way. "Where did you go? I wondered if you had walked out on me. They're very good shops they have here. Here, I got you a present too." She dropped her parcels on the front seat and handed me a paper bag.

"Did you settle us in?"

"Open it! Yes, in a funny little place. I took two singles, we'll both sleep better don't you agree? Do you like it?" The bag contained a dark blue beret. I leaned over to kiss her on her cheek. "Yes, it's nice. Very French."

"Isn't it? Even if it's from Taiwan. Put it on, let's see it."

"It won't go with a tuxedo."

"Don't you have a raincoat?" she asked.

"I left it in the Frankfurt Press club. They had locked it away."

"Why would they do that? Your stuff is in your room. Hotel Floréal, straight ahead a couple of blocks, you can't miss it, there's a neon sign. I'm going to look at some more shops, they told me to try the Uniprix which is like our Five-and-Ten but better. I know you hate that kind of thing." She started locking the car and waited for me to get out.

"Yes, I guess I do. Will I see you at the hotel? But you can't leave that car here."

"Sure I can. Tourists just get warnings on their windshields. Aren't I doing well here?"

"Very well." I put the beret on now. "Look." But she had already turned away.

My shoes sopping and sighing, I got to the Floréal, its neon sign showing a red rose. The bed buckled under my weight. It's good that she's done it this way, I really can't sleep too well in one bed with somebody else. God, everyone feels bad alone in a foreign hotel room, I always do. Except for that one night in Spain after the restaurant. Two-to-a-bed you are just as much less alone in the universe as you're nearer to God sitting on the spire of the cathedral.

Is that a political banner across the street? Maybe there'll be barricades tomorrow under these somber skies, that would help.

The narrow hotel window was very dirty and the rain had streaked it oddly in all directions, sideways too. I could make out only a few letters on the banner where the glass of the window had been washed clean, an X and two P's. The X intrigued me. I sat up and moved my head back and forth to read the rest of the letters through that peephole. The X turned out to belong to Luxe, as in Appartements-Prestige-Luxe which were going to be for sale here.

I took the only picture off the wall, I could just reach it, and lay down with it on the bed after blowing away the dust. It showed a girl and a little child in dresses of long ago under a tall tree. The girl was trying to reach an apple. "Souvenir de Mortefontaine" it said underneath. I stared at it until I became dizzy with wishing myself back into that time where I would have known the girl in the long skirt. She had since lived her life, she had grown old and died, uncomforted perhaps.

I wrote "Salle Martel" in soap on the mirror above the little sink.

I felt sorry for myself, sitting on the sinking bed in the now quickly darkening room.

31

Claire wanted another day in Strasbourg and I did not try to talk her out of it. I had my tuxedo cleaned at the Floréal and sold it together with the black shoes in a little tailor shop two blocks from the hotel. They gave me two hundred francs, less than the deposit I had left for it in Frankfurt, enough to follow the orchestra, to hitchhike to Paris without much worry. But I did not go ahead. Claire was blossoming, though, and I was wrong thinking that she would have minded.

In the dead of night, back in my room after our love making, tired and sleepless, I sat in the window sill and stared at the banner flapping in the wind. Supernatural darkness of Appartements-Prestige-Luxe floating across the tops of cities.

When I wrote "love making" I was being euphemistic: as I bent over her, she had held me back and said, "Just stroke me." She was in that sort of mood sometimes, it was exciting in its own way, and she reciprocated. But this time she had stayed motionless. I went on and on, she shook her head angrily, muttering, and finally she pushed my hand away and made herself come. I had put her hands on me then but it did not work. "You're not milking a cow," I said and she answered, "You better do it yourself," and turned her back on me.

It is a matter of power, she is the kind of person who respects power of whatever sort, she respects a man who knows how to make pizzas or who is a good carpenter. She has lost her respect for me because she thinks I'm just messing around. I wondered, again, how I could tell her about my search. She would fall silent and perhaps say, "It's not my kind of scene but more power to you ... I have underestimated you."

But the very beginning of my explanation already sounded wrong. "You never asked me what I was doing in Frankfurt," I said.

"What were you doing in Frankfurt?"

"If you really want to know—it is not easy to explain. Do you remember that Greece, Crete specifically, was a matriarchate once? Ruled under a female principle, God seen as a woman, the earth—"

"No, I don't remember," she broke in. "I wasn't around."

"Oh come on, Claire. I mean, remember from school."

"I took typing instead of Ancient civilizations."

A silence. Once more she didn't ask me to continue.

We had a fine last evening in Strasbourg, though, with a lot of wine, and she accepted without cynicism that I would repay her and that it was my treat. On the way back to the Floréal she became very quiet and I was going to tell her about the Romance of the Rose, for we had had a wine called Riquewhir and I had said that was the name of a knight. She used to like hearing about sensual but scholarly things. But suddenly we were already at the hotel, much sooner than I had thought (the neon Rose had been turned off), and she said, "I want to have a coffee by myself here, do you mind? I'll be up later." In the elevator I finally remembered that Floréal is the name of a month in the French Revolution. I lay awake but did not hear her come up.

The following morning was windy under a blue sky. I made my standard offer to drive which was as always rejected, and presently we were on the Autoroute to Paris.

"I liked that town," she said in a low voice.

I answered that she'd like Paris even more.

"Lucas," she asked, "how do you see yourself?"

"As a seeker of wisdom and truth," which was a tired joke of ours from a musical we had once seen together.

"Have you faced the fact that you're a loser?"

"Well, if it's the opposite of a yuppie, I don't mind."

It was like a return to old times when she'd attack me in little ways, I usually wasn't sure why. I produced a little laugh. "If a loser is a man on a raft and the rest of you are in the first-class cabins of the Titanic—Here." I put a wad of bank notes between us on the seat.

She didn't look away from the road. "Money? What is it?"

"A thousand francs. Two hundred dollars more or less. Your loan. The rest will follow."

"How did you get that?"

"Ha. The Floréal did cash my check."

She looked down at the money and then at me but didn't say anything more.

When I close my eyes I can see ourselves in the little rented car as if from the outside; the car is some kind of pastel pink, a pink blot racing down the almost empty white thruway in a grey landscape under a light sky, Claire going 140 kilometers an hour, the high wind whistling at whatever knobs or bits of the car stick out.

But when we had entered Paris (and she drove the whole way without stopping except at the toll booths), she pulled over at a crossroads of boulevards and said, "I think we should split here," and I wasn't taken aback and didn't argue. I immediately got my bag from the rear seat, kissed her on her cheek, and was off. Halfway down the block I passed the sign of a little hotel and walked in without hesitation, closing its door behind me. If she changed her mind and felt sorry for me, I didn't want her to come after me when the light turned green.

They had a room and I sat there a while. I still had the two hundred francs from the tuxedo and later I went out to buy rolls and an apple. On my way back I took a newspaper from a chair in the hotel corridor up to my room and used my nail scissors to cut out letters from it, the way blackmailers do. I was starting a letter to the Frankfurt police, telling them that Dr. Vinograd had presumably drowned his wife in the seas off Comillas on the north shore of Spain.

I did this because everything was becoming shadowy and I needed to see "Dr. Vinograd" and "Comillas" in printed letters, lined up by me. Once I had seen that, I cut the word "presumably" out of the letter.

32

Two hours later I sat in the Salle Martel waiting for the concert to start. I had bought the cheapest ticket, twenty francs, but the hall was not very deep and I wasn't more than sixty feet or so from the podium. I had bought no program and did not know what music to expect and I did not know what it would mean to see her, the woman from Comillas, on the stage. Seeing her play a violin or a flute might make me realize she was simply a musician and a woman, an exceptionally beautiful woman but precisely because of that without the remotest link with me. And the watchman at the artists' entrance wouldn't let me through if I presented myself afterward in my green suit. The tuxedo would have served better, but the green suit would have fetched more like twenty than like two hundred francs. Anyway, I liked having to wear it without choice or alternative. It was not a suit you chose in the morning, it was a fateful suit.

A few men and women were on stage now, tuning their instruments halfheartedly, not helped by the freezing temperature in the hall. It may have been my empty stomach at the end of the day rather than nerves but I began to feel shaky and had to get off my uncomfortable chair. I went back out to the corridor where I found a sofa. It was better, sitting there, and I must even have fallen asleep, for an attendant touching my shoulder startled me. I did not understand his words and then he repeated in English that if I did not go in, I would have to wait for—and then followed a name I did not catch. "Second movement?" he said, waving two fingers.

His concern was comforting but my legs were very weak. "I'll wait for that," I said, "I came only for that second movement." I had to control myself firmly in order not to start shivering. I put my hands in my pockets and sat up very straight.

The first piece or movement was short. There was applause, and the attendant who had remained beside the curtained door, gave me a nod which well-nigh forced me to get up and shuffle into the concert hall.

It was warmer in there now and quite full. I sat down on a chair at the back rather than make people get up for me, and finally turned my eyes to the stage just as the lights in the hall dimmed.

A strange music began. It was somber yet southern, Mediterranean, plaintive, nostalgic—I do not know enough about music to describe it properly. I did not forget why I was there and the music, which swayed between overwhelming and whispering, made what I was doing seem sensible once more. It was music from a world where irrationality was not mad but wise.

It took a while before I dared scrutinize the musicians but my vision was far from clear and I could not make them out at all. The long movement, symphony, whatever it was, ended in a painful, almost inaudible, dying music. The audience sat silently, then began to clap. Some men in the audience stood up and shouted, "Bravo!" I stood too and walked forward, and only when I stood beside the front row of seats did I stand still and look up. All the lights were on now and the members of the orchestra were on their feet, bowing. An attendant brought bouquets to the women. I let my eyes travel from one side to the other, I studied their faces which were not listless now but absent, melancholy rather than happy. She was not among them.

My heart started beating more slowly. I caught my breath, I felt I had been granted a stay, more time.

33

In the intermission I did go backstage and as for once I wasn't worried about the impression I made, they didn't stop me. I found some of the musicians sitting around a table drinking wine or instant coffee made on the spot with an electric kettle. There were also people not dressed in evening clothes. No one paid attention to my entrance. I heard the word "arrangement" in French a large number of times. Two men were smoking cigarettes with their legs up, reading newspapers.

I pulled out my clipping from the Rhine newspaper and went over to the table. An older woman whom I recognized as a cellist looked at me and I apologized for the intrusion, but could she help me? Wasn't this woman in the photograph a member of the orchestra? And where was she now?

She took the piece of paper from me.

"I've come all the way to Paris just to find her," I added.

She passed the picture on to the man next to her and shook her head. "I do remember the face," she said, "but—What's her name?"

"I don't know."

"You've come to Paris all the way from where? To find a woman whose name you do not know?"

"It sounds odd, I guess."

She smiled. "La grande passion," she said.

Her neighbor gave me back the picture, shaking his head too.

"She was never in the orchestra then?"

"She traveled with us, I have seen her," the cellist said. "She kept to herself. I thought she was perhaps standing in for someone or working as an impresario. I never saw her after Strasbourg. Maria, is that her name? Mind you, I'm not sure. And this is not a very clear picture."

She showed it to someone else at the table, a young man busy opening a bottle.

"Maria," he said. "That odd person with the odd face." He spoke English, with a strong accent I could not place.

Several of them were now studying the clipping. "Odd? Not odd, she was beautiful. Strangely beautiful," a girl said.

The picture came back to me and the general conversation started again. I went over to the girl. "Do you perhaps know her last name," I asked, "or where she is now?"

"We never talked. But I saw her in Paris our first day here, I am sure of that. She joined us in Germany, for a little while. She didn't share our hotels."

"She was too clever for that," the young man added. "Or as you say, too beautiful. No fleabag places for her."

"We're not doing so badly," the girl answered him.

"We aren't?" And, looking at me, "We are doing repulsivo. You understand repulsivo?"

I nodded.

In the meantime, a security guard in uniform whom I had not noticed, had posted himself next to me and he now made a gesture for me to follow him out. I looked at the company but no one intervened and thus I bowed at them, sort of, and obeyed. Starting back through the long corridor toward the concert hall itself, I noticed an exit door where a porter stood smoking a cigarette. Beyond him lay the gleaming asphalt of the boulevard along which dead leaves were pushed by the wind. A strange, painful emotion got me in its grip, and made me rush through that door, past the porter, out into the street.

34

Lucas stood still at the edge of the pavement and looked up and down the boulevard. He had been blind to it on his way to the concert hall. He now thought it looked festive and welcoming, under a sky reflecting the soft glow of the street lamps and the yellow waves of car headlights.

He wondered if Maria was her real name. It was a good name to think of her, too basic and universal to conjure up false connotations. How strange it was! As if she had materialized in this odd photograph, posing with the orchestra, only to prove she was not a fantasy. He pulled out the clipping and studied it again in the strong light from a shop window, he stared at it until it dissolved once more into its black and white dots. He had to cup it with his hands as if it were a burning candle to shelter it from the wind, because the paper was fragile and already yellowing. Tomorrow he could—but what was there left to do tomorrow, what was there left to wait for? He had come near. He had approached another world he knew nothing of; he had, different from the members of this orchestra or the diners in the Spanish restaurant, been aware of the mystery of her. He had been given a chance but had failed to grab it; at some point he had been insufficient. If he had followed her train that morning, somehow, on foot if need be, instead of traveling in comfort in a little free-mileage rented car? But he did not try to pull his contradictory thoughts together.

A boy bumped into him and the newspaper clipping blew away. He dived after it, retrieved it before it had reached a puddle, and dabbed it with his handkerchief. He looked at it and even from a foot away it was just black and white dots. He opened his hand and let it blow away once more. He sat down in a doorway.

A strange figure, this un-American American of uncertain age in the terrible green suit, sitting on the doorstop of a closed baking shop as he let go of a face fading from his memory. He was staring at the evening life of the boulevard with its conflicting civilizations of mysterious beauty and equally mysterious ugliness which had once so attracted generations of young men from America (come to spend their lives here in a never-ending misunderstanding), civilizations almost gone under now, weighed down by the late twentieth century. A passer-by, for some reason touched by the look in his staring eyes, felt in his pocket for change. Only finding a twenty-franc bill, he nevertheless dropped the note in Lucas' lap. Perhaps he was slightly drunk or was going home after a lovely rendezvous; it was that hour.

35

The night man at the hotel unbolted the front door for me and brought me a waterglass half-full of cognac in exchange for a twenty-franc note begged by me (effortlessly) in the street. That helped. Right above my head was an old wall telephone and I started considering a call to my New York bookstore. I had to look ahead, hadn't I, owning all of a hundred francs, my charter ticket probably worthless now, and my job already lost. I couldn't for the life of me remember how much leave the manager had given me and which illness I had claimed to have. In the dim light of the hallway I sat and stared at the rack with curled-up tourist brochures, the map of the Paris metro held up by three thumb tacks, the airline posters.

I stood up to go crawl into my bed, and sat down again. One o'clock in Paris was a favorable hour to call. The manager would have gone home, it would be so much easier to deal with someone else, Jos if I were lucky. It was seven in the evening there.

Here goes, collect to New York City. Bless him, I recognized Jos' voice. He hesitated. "It's a matter of life and death!" I cried right through the operator's voice, and he took the call.

"Jos, do I still have my job?"

"To be perfectly frank, I doubt it. A new girl came in last week."

"Shit. Can you tell Mrs. Blum that I've been terribly ill, I couldn't call before. I had pneumonia, I was almost a goner. Honestly."

"Salmonella poisoning, she told me."

"Pneumonia. I can prove it. I'll be back in one or two days. Tell her I count on her."

"Okay. Okay, I'll try. But I wouldn't get my hopes up if I were you. Blumski is not going to fire this new chick."

I did not know what to answer.

"Lucas, okay? I'll do my best. Keep cool now."

I was standing there, listening to the New York silence I was returning to.

"Wait, don't hang up," I cried.

"Hurry, I'll be fired for taking this call," Jos said. "I'll be right behind you in that bread line."

"Do you still want my apartment?"

"What? Are you serious?" He wasn't in a hurry anymore.

"You can sublet it from me. Five hundred dollars a month. That's what I pay."

"Are you serious?" he repeated.

"I'll mail you the keys tomorrow, special delivery. No need to tell anyone. The landlord lives in Atlanta or somewhere. I'll write you the poop. But you must wire me two months' rent, tomorrow, to American Express Paris."

"I haven't got a thousand dollars at the moment."

"Well, at least one month. As much as you can. Promise."

"I promise."

"Okay then. You'll have the keys before Monday. Just put my stuff in the hall closet."

"Wait," he now said. "What about you? Where are you going? What do I say to Blum?"

"Nothing. Don't say anything. Don't forget, American Express Paris. You promised."

I sat down under the phone. I counted my money, a hundred and twenty francs left. Never mind, I wasn't going to bed now, I was going out and eat dinner.

I had given myself one more chance. "I saw her in Paris," the girl in the Salle Martel had said.

36

I was up at dawn. The brightness of a city dawn which remains unknown to its citizens: they start waking up and staring out of their small bathroom windows into streets when the sky has clouded over and rain is about to fall for the day.

I had to prod the same watchman of the night before in order to have him unlock the front door. Out under that tight blue sky I wandered down empty streets. I tried the door of a bakery still closed although they had lights on, came to another bakery where a woman in a freshly ironed white coat was selling dozens of long thin loaves to a man in a T-shirt. Instead of buying a roll, I bought one of those loaves too. The man in the T-shirt nodded at me as he passed, holding his loaves in his red, scrubbed, hands; outside he tied them on the back of a scooter. I observed all this with interest.

I ate my bread as I went along without bothering where I was going. I didn't get tired. When later the streets became rainy and crowded, I asked the way to American Express where I was the first customer when they unlocked the doors. I never doubted that Jos' money was waiting for me, but when the man told me there was nothing, I realized my stupidity. It was still night in New York.

When the money came, I'd take up my search. Clues would present themselves; the toughest barrier was my own fear of finding her, and discovering it had all been a madness. I sat on park benches and it rained and rained. A watery sun appeared. I ate another loaf of bread but of course it wasn't as good as that first one. Finally I made my way back to the hotel and called the Salle Martel from the pay phone in the hallway. I got the name of the person who had been in charge of the Chicago orchestra. He or she would be in later in the day. I think that's what they told me.

Behind the reception desk of the hotel a woman was doing paperwork and staring at me a lot. I asked for my key, expecting trouble, and sure enough she asked me to settle the bill so far, the hotel had a rule—"Yes, of course," I said, "I'll be right back, I forgot to mail this letter," waving my anonymous denunciation to the Frankfurt police. Then I turned around and left.

I went to sit in the metro station across the road. It was nice and warm, but time moved so slowly that it made me think of my night in the zoo. I tried to keep my mind on that owl with its eyes wide open. Stop-time immortality. Two policemen strolled by and then turned around and asked me something in what sounded like an attempt at German. That was because of my green suit, no doubt; under the fluorescent light I looked like a lost Black Forest backwoodsman, a junior Hitler. Maybe they'd beat me up in order to prevent World War Three. But I got up and left and no one did anything.

Out on the boulevard I talked to some girls (one looked about twelve years old). Images of a woman's body drifted through my mind, not Claire's, no one's, a body, womanhood. They all asked to see my money before taking me anywhere, out of the rain. After that, boys came and showed me little packets of stuff in the palms of their hands, a new gesture to me, but no doubt it's ubiquitous too now.

Around four or so I went back to the American Express place and I made them check twice, but there was nothing there. Twelve francs left, not enough to telephone Jos. I could call collect once more, but I'd have to wait. Damn, there was nothing I could sell, and here I had mailed Jos those keys, special delivery, quite expensive. I looked at myself in the mirror of a shop entrance and spruced myself up. Then I set out for the Salle Martel. The porter let me in without any fuss and I found the manager, a woman, in an office full of people coming and going. There was an empty chair in the back of the room where I sat down. Under the seat stood a half-empty carton of coffee, which I finished. Behind the window of a house across, a little pale girl stood staring at me. I waved and she waved back.

37

It became quiet in the room and I went up to the desk. A middle-aged woman sat there, very chic, in a low black dress; I sort of bowed and said I was Lucas Iberia who had called before. I was trying to find a woman who had worked or traveled with the Chicago Orchestra. Her name was Maria.

Behind her, a man appeared through an another door, a stack of papers in his hand. The woman held out her hand for the papers but looked at me and asked, "Maria? What is her full name?" She picked up a pencil.

"I only know, Maria."

The pencil landed back on her desk. "The Salle Martel is not a dating service, unfortunately," she said, but not really nastily.

"It isn't like that at all."

"Oh?" But I had clearly lost her attention. She put the papers in front of her and appeared to be waiting for me to leave. Several people came in through the door behind me and I understood her to ask, in French, "Anyone here knows a Maria in the Chicago orchestra?"

They didn't, the phone rang, and they all started talking. I began to leave, but passing the empty chair, I decided to wait a bit longer. Through the wall I could hear the same music they had performed the night before, when I was at the concert, the same music rebelling against logic. It gave me a certain new courage.

When everyone had trouped out again, she saw me sit there and said in a loud voice, "You're still here." She didn't seem as annoyed as I had expected.

I smiled at her. "Perhaps Maria is not her real name," I said. "More a nom de guerre, you see."

"I don't see what you expected me—Yes!"

That "Yes" was in response to a knock on the door. Two men came in, involved in a heated conversation. They stopped it to greet her and sat down in front of her desk.

"Before we begin," she told them in English, "can anyone help this gentleman? He is looking for a Maria from the Chicago orchestra."

They turned around and looked at me, one blandly, the other with what seemed an angry frown. I stood up. They both shook their heads.

"Well, there you are," she said. "Now you must leave us be, please."

"Just one question," I hastily said. "What was it they played just now?" I pointed at the wall.

"Didn't you say you were a musician?"

"No. I didn't. I'm a forester."

Luckily she ignored that. "It was De Falla. Spanish music."

I don't know where all I went from there, the air full of rain enveloping me; I was no longer miserable and I wasn't happy; I was above those feelings. It was a long night, and much became clear. Men and women, girls, whores, boys with drugs, looked at me but no one spoke a word. Neither did I.

In the beginning was not, the word. In the beginning was the earth, a golden age of softness, not soft weak, but soft harmonious, naked nymphs instead of armored Roman goddesses, Nibelungen extras.

With the word, the male world started. And under the flags of words, war, slaughter, enslaving began.

I'm dizzy with hunger, I admit it, but I am not insane. I recognized the woman in Comillas as if she were a link to that golden age. Humor me, I tell everyone, if soundlessly. If such an idea saves me, why ever not.

When I came to, so to speak, when I noticed myself wandering, wet, unshaven, and all the rest of it, it had long since dawned. I got myself a free metro ride, I had seen others do that, you push right behind some other passenger going through the automatic doors, and you ignore the dirty looks they give you. I had to get back into my hotel, if only to change; I'd tell them of the money on its way to me.

There was a different man behind the reception desk, someone I had not seen before. I began my little rehearsed speech but he interrupted me. Pointing at a man sitting in the chair under the wall phone, he said, "A visitor for you." And to the man, in French, "That's him."

38

"You came to see *me?*" I asked him

He nodded. "From the Salle Martel." He spoke English in a hoarse, accented voice. Spanish, maybe.

"My room is being cleaned. We can have a coffee next door."

He took a table in the back of the café. He looked a man of thirty or so, in a dark blue raincoat which was too big for him, a rough face but not the face of a bully. He seemed to eye me with suspicion or hostility, though.

The café had a pile of napkins on the counter. I went over to get a bunch of them, put them on the floor, and after getting out of my shoes rubbed my wet feet on them. I stuffed some in each shoe. My visitor paid no attention to this, nor to my dripping hair or three-day beard; he seemed to be waiting for me to ask a question. But I could not think of one. I have always been a suspicious person but not now. Perhaps my night on the street had freed me from that. And since I had mailed off my apartment key, I had nothing left that anyone could want.

I put as much milk and sugar in my coffee as the cup could master and gulped it down. It lessened my dizziness but I felt a hundred years old. "May I have another coffee?" I asked him, although he hadn't suggested the first one was on him.

He ordered me another coffee and a bottle of mineral water for himself. In French, he indeed rolled his r's like a man from the south.

"You showed up at the right time," I said.

"How so?"

"I was dying for a cup of coffee."

He frowned. Whatever he had expected of me, I didn't seem to fit the part. "That man at the reception acted very strange when I asked for you," he informed me.

"A misunderstanding. A misunderstanding I had with the hotel."

"And you're an American?"

"Born in Boston. On Joy Street."

He gave me a tired little smile. He thought I was trying to be funny. "And your name is Iberria?"

I nodded just in time. The disadvantage of my many names, the only disadvantage I may say, is that I don't always remember them in time. I had borrowed the name Iberia when I registered at the hotel; I borrowed it from a tattered airline poster on the wall. The poster didn't show any planes, by the way, only a very luscious girl under a palm tree.

"How did you know?" I asked but I was really concentrating on the waiter who stood chatting at the counter instead of bringing me coffee.

"Well, from the Salle Martel," he said.

"Oh. Of course." I now recognized him as one of the men in the manager's office. The one with the angry frown.

"Your hotel, too," he added. "All on the visitor's slip the porter fills out."

Finally my coffee. This time I left out the milk or cream which had been slightly sickening, but put in the more sugar. I don't like it but it's nourishment.

He cleared his throat, to make me look at him, I think, and then he said loudly, "Arbeiten Sie für Herr Vinograd?", which of course is German for, "Are you working for Mr. Vinograd?"

This took me by surprise all right, so much so that I needed some seconds to change the meaningless sounds into words in another language, German, that is. I think I stood up, I'm not quite sure about that. I was bewildered for certain. "What the fuck—," I muttered. "Is this a trick? Is that asshole still after me? What the hell?", or words to that effect.

More staring from him. Then he asked, "You don't like Mr. Vinograd?"

"Like? He set the police on me. He had me deported. He—But what is this all about? Who are you? What the hell?"

My indignation seemed to please him, he seemed to look less hostile. "Maybe, I was wrong about something," he said, more to himself than to me. "I guess I was. It's all very complicated. You are broke, aren't you?"

"Temporarily. Yes."

"Maybe we have a job for you, a little job to help you out. Come see me at the Salle Martel tomorrow, I have my office there. Okay? Say, nine o'clock?"

I wondered what to answer.

"I'll explain it all. Don't worry. Here, you can have a little advance. A man can't live on coffee with sugar only." He smiled and handed me a hundred-franc note. "Tomorrow morning then?"

Why ever not. "Okay," I said. "But—"

He waited.

"Could you—if it's an advance, could you make it five hundred francs? I have some problems to iron out, with my hotel."

He didn't look too pleased but he muttered "Como no," which means, why not.

I stayed the rest of the morning in the café, going through a lot of his money on coffees and sandwiches. I looked in their mirrors now and saw I had a face of something the cat had dragged in, as we used to say, but in the end I went back to the hotel. They weren't very gracious and my new solvency didn't impress them. My old room was no longer free, they told me. There was another one, but it was twenty-five francs more.

"Fine, fine. And let me have my suitcase if you please."

This new room looked out on a wall and was worse than the old one. I hung up my suit to dry and wrapped myself in the blanket.

39

The idea of pain often occupied Lucas' thoughts. Not a fear of pain for himself, but the idea that only humans inflicted it, not as an involuntary complement to hunting and being hunted for food, but to bend others to their will. He had read about the famous cases of torture in history, such as the execution in the eighteenth century of Damiens, a bewildered friar who had scratched Louis the Fifteenth of France with a penknife as the king was about to step into his coach. His death became the most detailed of the century, for the king convened a conference of physicians who drew up a plan for the slowest possible killing of the friar. To watch such torture was a voluptuous pleasure for the people in those days, and perhaps it is again becoming such in our time.

The evening of his meeting with Miguel he had been wandering through the town, different from before, for he was dry and full of food, finally a real tourist, as he told himself. But when he crossed a large square (the Place de l'Hotel de Ville), he suddenly had started to shiver. Just then a torrential rain set in. The Place de l'Hotel de Ville was once the Place de Grève, where the citizens of Paris came to watch executions. European cities all have such squares. Possibly an electronic microscope could still discover traces of blood, of sinews and of bone marrow, between the cobblestones of those places. Lucas, shivering, imagined he heard screaming. He stood still, and a lady who was just going to take a photograph of her husband beside the fountain (in spite of the rain), bumped into him. Lucas didn't know the history of the spot where he was standing and that here the Damiens executioner had put up his rack. His hearing those screams cannot be explained as autosuggestion.

The following morning I felt very low. I had caught a cold, wandering through town and getting caught in an icy downpour, but that wasn't it. The unease of Spain was creeping back up on me. I told myself seeing Miguel might help, for there was a link here though I didn't yet understand it; he knew of the man, Vinograd I mean, and he knew of her. Once in the metro to the Salle Martel, I began to feel better, but that was because of a North African on the train who played the flute for us.

As he came down the aisle for money, I watched people's reaction. Some looked away or shook their heads, but others, especially women, even poor ones, searched through their pockets or in crammed handbags for change. I gave him five francs, which was quite a bit of money for me just then.

I was thinking of a summer evening when a man was playing just such a flute coming down our street in Boston, stopping every few steps to look up at the houses. My mother made me get her purse and threw him a quarter wrapped in a piece of paper. The musician nearly caught it in midair but then he had to bend heavily to pick it up. He lifted his hat to us, a shapeless black hat, and I ducked under the window sill because I was embarrassed at him seeing me, embarrassed for him, that is. And afterward I felt inconsolable, my mother couldn't figure out why and I guess I didn't know myself.

Perhaps because we are such piteous creatures, I now think, or at best a hair's breadth away from piteousness. And there's so little pity. But without pity our lives and our deaths are unbearable. I wouldn't have been able to put that in words then, but I knew it in my guts. Here I sat, looking out the window and staring at the little lights flying by in the dark metro tunnel, having trouble keeping my tears back.

It was an odd talk I had with this man Miguel, more like a police interview with all the questions he asked. It got me a foot on dry land, though. I mean my black-and-white (memories of old movies) search took on some color. Enough to make a new man out of me, or as near as dammit.

First Miguel had kept me waiting in his office, a little room with a bare desk. Nothing much to see there but a photograph on his desk, a picture of a television screen it seemed, a picture twice removed from reality. It showed a man in a dark suit, a striped suit, with on each side a man in uniform. It was not very clear, it was all grey lines, but the men looked like bodyguards or some kind of escort. Maybe they were arresting the man in the suit. A piece of balustrade stuck out in a corner which could equally well be the edge of a balcony from which this man was going to address the voters or the scaffolding of a gallows from which he was going to be hanged.

I had the strange idea that Miguel had kept me waiting here with the picture on purpose, to frighten me.

"So are you a Basque then," his voice behind me said. I put the photograph back on the desk.

"Aren't you?" he asked.

"I was born in Boston, USA."

He shook his head. "Yes, yes. I mean of course your father, your origin. I've known several Iberrias in Spain. Some of them are from the Béarn, on this side of the border. But they're all Basques."

Well, I am the son of an airline poster.

"Do you still speak the language?" he asked. "Any words at all?" He wanted me to say yes, I could tell.

"Eh—my parents were leery of the subject, my mother was. When my father started on it, she always shut him up."

"Why was that?"

Why. "I guess the subject frightened her. She had lived through the bad days when Franco sent those masons to the cemeteries to chisel away any Basque words—She ran there to stop them. In the end they smashed her parents' tombstone, she was lucky they didn't do anything to her. She came home with the pieces in her scarf. Some of the pieces. That was before I was born, of course."

Miguel nodded. "What I figured, more or less. Maybe those weren't such bad days, Iberria. Everyone knew where everyone stood."

So far so good. I enjoyed this. I've done little but reading history all my life, I could go on with this for hours, give that Basque father hands without nails from when he was tortured by the fascists, an uncle hiding out in our attic for ten years, you name it, I provide it. But better leave well enough alone, perhaps. "And so?" was all I said then.

"Sit down. Cigarette?"

I shook my head.

"Listen carefully. I came after you because you were inquiring after Maria. People who do that, we cut their throats."

I made a face. He didn't sound convincing in this role.

"We would," Miguel said. "It hasn't happened so far."

"You know her then?"

"No one *knows* her. I have seen her. From a distance."

"Is she a Basque too?" I couldn't think of anything else to ask right then.

"Maria? Have you ever seen a Basque looking like that?" He didn't wait for me to answer. "She is Vinograd's enemy, and that's all we have to know. I've made enquiries, I know the chief clerk at the police headquarters of Frankfurt, Germany." He said that very slowly.

"So?"

"So, I don't know what you want with Maria. I don't have to know, but I'm satisfied you're on our side. I'll vouch for you."

"Vouch? With whom?"

"You're broke, aren't you?"

"Temporarily."

He shook his head impatiently. "Cut the crap, Iberria. There's no time for that. We have a job next week and I need another hand. In the meantime, you can help load and unload musical instruments here at the Salle. That'll keep you in coffee, with lots of sugar."

Well, he smiled as he said that, so why not smile back. I didn't have a clue what he was about and if he thought I was going to throw a bomb for them or something like that, he was very mistaken. But to earn some money was essential.

Miguel sent me to the post office with bundles of Salle Martel programs after this. It was quite a load, really too heavy for one man, but I ambled down the avenue with it, looking every passer-by in the face and some women or perhaps all of them smiled back at me. I was surely visible. I didn't remember ever having felt that particular sharp, sense of triumph. Admit it, triumph over a hell of a lot of odds, you'll have to cut that act about always having such bad luck. One girl looked at me, so expectant almost, that I put my bundles down on a window sill, pulled out a Salle Martel flyer, and handed it to her. She had waited for it, it didn't matter what it was.

How strange to be in a mood for which I could think of no example in our image-drowned world, a mood out of sync with my time. All I must do now is, to measure up. To deserve this.

Most of that night I sat in my chair near the window of the hotel room, looking out on the wall. The lights from other rooms made oblongs on the yellowish bricks and I started betting on them; if the top one would go off before the middle one it would be a good omen and vice versa. But I fell asleep in the chair and when I woke up, all the lights had gone out. Good. Never mind an omen. Measure up.

41

From the balcony of a boarding house I was looking out over blue-tiled roofs into a blue sky. Warm sun, stone walls warm to the touch. We had come here by train, St. Jean in the south of France near the Spanish border, four of us. Miguel was in charge but he had stayed in Paris.

Across the valley of rooftops I could see the sign of a resort hotel, "Hotel Edouard VII," in 1900-style square letters. Most of the town was in that 1900 mold when overweight men and women came here to drink the water from the source and air their nubile daughters in the process. Only the mold was left now, inside it were discos and pizzerias. The 1900 certainties had vanished, and what a short timespan the whole melodrama had had! From King Edward II who was taught a lesson when they stuck a white-hot poker up his innards (his scream could be heard at the castle gate a mile away) to King Edward VII whose pleasures weren't punished but depicted in *The Tatler and Bystander*, it had all been but one beat in the Cenozoic Period. My father wore the same beige spats Edward VII did. In fact, that's about the only thing I remember of my father.

The four of us were here, in Miguel's words, for an act of public theater, nothing more. Just as in London they close off certain alleyways to retain a private right of way, thus we were going to close the Basque borders for an hour, or for as long as we got away with it. "Once the Spanish custom posts were as far south as the Ebro River," he had announced. It was the kind of thing that got the attention of the media.

As far as I was concerned, it was the kind of thing we did in school in 1968 or so, and I had no great urge to take it up again. Still, I had expected worse, and since Miguel saw it as a kind of test for me, I was certainly going to do my best to please him. As for now, after a long season in the rain so to speak, here I was sitting on a balcony in the late afternoon sun, warm and dry for the first time in months. No complaints.

42

On the morning of their action Lucas and a man whose name he understood to be Scargo were dropped off at a stone bridge on an empty country road. A sign in white and blue gave the name of the river as the Nive. It formed the northern border of Basque territory in France, he was told, and they had to see to it that at precisely seven a.m. the road across the bridge was blocked. "Not a living soul will notice," Lucas said, looking out over the road and the bare fields. It was half past five in the morning and fog enveloped the landscape.

Scargo spoke better English than Lucas French, and he was in charge. On each side of the road they were to make a series of holes at the bottom of the poplars, fit plastic explosives with mercury-fused detonators in them, and make the trees topple into the road. Scargo also had signs with him announcing in French, Spanish, and Basque the closing of the Euzkadi border. They took turns drilling; the wood was moist and very tough.

The whine of the battery-powered drill was loud in the mist. They started, stopped, listened, but there was no echo, no sound of traffic, nothing. The road stretched arrow-straight into the distance, the two lines of poplars making a perfect tunnel. It is a pity for these lovely trees.

Lucas must have spoken the words aloud for Scargo looked at him and shrugged, "Someone will be happy with the firewood," he remarked. "They are poor here."

The mist began to lift and a little red sunlight filtered through. Scargo took metal wedges out of his backpack and showed Lucas how to hammer them in, to make sure the trees would fall in the right direction. Working beside him, a sense of well-being filled Lucas, the sense of having a place within the scheme of things, of belonging, even in something as simple as the hammering away with another man at tree trunks. He was not quite aware of its cause.

Scargo put in the explosives. "We've half an hour," he said, "let's have a cigarette." They went to sit on the parapet of the bridge.

"Have you done this before?" Lucas asked.

"I've worked with explosives, they're tricky. You have to learn. I have never done this. It is a new idea. Here comes somebody. Don't jump, just smoke your cigarette." A white van had become visible, it flashed by and disappeared. "Spanish license plate," Scargo said.

"It's not exactly a busy crossing."

"We have the easiest, it's your first time. The others have the route D 20 to Irun, that one is tricky."

"Suppose no one else comes along all day?"

Scargo shrugged. "We have the press release."

"No kidding?"

"But of course. This is a political action. Otherwise, there's no point."

"In the sixties—," Lucas began but Scargo had jumped into the road.

"It is the moment," he told Lucas. "I will do the left row, you do the right row. Perforate each cell, quickly, as I show you." He gave him a two-inch nail.

These detonators have two compartments with a waxed cardboard separation, and a hole in it sets the chemical reaction into motion.

They were back on the bridge at the same time. "All done," Scargo said. "Oh—Merde!"

A flickering red light had appeared far off on the road, incorporeal in the mist still caught between the trees.

"Fous le camp," Scargo whispered. "It is the police."

As they started running, the first explosion sounded, not very loud. Turning, Lucas saw a tree, the one on the left closest to the bridge, begin toppling over. The police car, now of a sudden incomprehensibly near, braked sharply but the tree hit it on the roof with a sickening whack.

Whether by accident or design, the car's siren began to howl. In the same instant that the driver jumped out, a tree on the other side of the road, Lucas' side, started tilting although Lucas had heard no explosion. He stared across the bridge at the police officer, a man with a frowning, oldish face and a russet mustache who had stretched out his hand as if pointing at him. They faced each other, immobile, as the tree hit the policeman and knocked him to the ground.

Lucas turned and ran on. That endless moment had been less than a second; Scargo was only some twelve feet ahead of him down the road and he immediately caught up with him. "Can't you go faster?" he panted.

"Oh fuck you. Fuck you. I can't run. I have bad sore on my ass."

A cramped laugh rose in Lucas' throat and died soundlessly. Should he run on or was he supposed to stick with this man whom he had never seen until a few hours ago? Stay on the road or make for the woods beyond the plowed fields? The wail of the police siren froze his mind, a weary and total hopelessness took hold of him. Mistakes never to be undone. He stood on the edge of the asphalt ribbon and said to Scargo, "You go on." Then he stepped into the ditch beside the road and lay down with his face against the whitish earth.

43

Miguel was smoking his cigarette in his Salle Martel office, not visibly pleased to see me, but very formal. He didn't know what role I had played at the border crossing, I thought. I wasn't too sure myself.

Weird as it may sound, in that ditch beside the bridge road I had fallen asleep. Or perhaps passed out. It was hours later when I opened my eyes to a pale sky. I lay there a while, light-headed, the hard and cold lumps of earth sticking into my back. The feeling of hopelessness which had put me there was as remote now as my well-being when I was working on the trees with Scargo. I was "neutral," I guess.

I got to my feet and faced an empty road. The air felt mild but humid, I slowly walked up the bridge and discovered the felled poplars still there, dragged just far enough apart to make a passage for a car. Nothing stirred.

I turned and made for Espelette, the village where according to the plan we would have been picked up at half past seven that morning. I found it an ugly little place with new cement houses and an irritating nervousness in the air, and I got on the first rural bus I saw in the central square. It ended its run at Bayonne where I took a stop train to Bordeaux and on to Paris. I hadn't enough money for the fast trains and sat through twelve hours on one of those sticky plastic seats, worse than the wooden third-class benches I remembered from my first summer in Europe.

Miguel had already told me that "my friend" had been arrested and was in a prison hospital. "We made our escapes separately," I answered.

"The man from the border police is in the Val de Grace hospital here in Paris," Miguel said. "He's in a coma, they flew him here, it is the place for brain surgery. This morning's *Figaro* says he will die and that all Basque agitators in France must be rounded up as accomplices in his murder."

A silence between us. He sounded as if he hadn't been the one to organize this.

"So much for your public theater," I said.

"Nothing like this was supposed to happen. I cannot afford such mistakes. I'm not blaming you, mind. As for your friend Snail, he is always too hasty."

"Snail?"

"Snail," he repeated with irritation. "His nickname. Escargot. Because he is too hasty."

"He wasn't, it was just as you had planned it. It is the fault of your damn press release."

"That did not go out till afterward. The police car was a coincidence. Life is nothing but a web of coincidences. Experience means expecting the unexpectable."

"I see." And fuck you, you self-satisfied bastard. "And as for this Snail—" I was going to say that he was no friend of mine but I stopped myself. He had felt like a friend when we were smoking our cigarettes on the bridge. Why not claim one friend.

"I'm not blaming you," Miguel repeated. "Actually you did well, getting back here unobserved, as far as we know. What we don't know is the leads they may have. Snail is discreet if anything, but poor devil, he's in pain, he has an anthrax."

"Yes."

He scrutinized my face, surprised, I guess, at what I've called my neutrality. All I felt was a diffuse disappointment. Neither Paris nor Miguel were familiar, the way they had seemed to be when I was on my way back here on those slow, slow trains.

"Perhaps you'd better get out of this city for a while," he said. "Can we still count on you?"

For what. But I nodded.

"Good. Good. You be off then, let things simmer down, I can let you have another five hundred francs, another loan."

I had earned the first five hundred but did not comment on that. He counted out the money and put it in front of me. "So where will you be?" he asked.

Where indeed. "There was a television photograph on your desk," I said instead.

He was busy counting the remaining money in his wallet and did not look at me as he answered, "What photograph? I never put photographs on my desk. I have no family."

"Me neither."

"Perhaps you should go back home all the same. To the U.S., I mean. We may be able to use you there."

"You said that before, but use me for what? How? Paid or unpaid, public theater or sudden death? I am here because I tried to find, to find someone. Or really, simply to see her one more time."

"And it's because of that, that we took you on. Look at yourself. Can you think of another reason? But maybe it's time to ask you, why exactly do you want to find her? What do you want from her?"

"I don't want anything from her. I just have to see her once more."

"Why?"

And I answered, words speaking themselves, "Because she is my last hope."

There was a long silence. Somehow he seemed to like and to accept that answer. His attitude toward me changed. He said softly, "Working for us, working with us, is working for her." He sat up straight and put out his cigarette. I think we both felt different then, his office looked less crummy, our stubbly faces less tired.

"What we want to do is not about borders," he said. "It is about justice."

"When you're born in Boston, it's hard to get very hot under the collar about the fight of the Basques," I told him.

"It is not about the Basques either. Perhaps it is about all injustice. Now and back through the centuries."

I smiled uneasily.

"This, Iberria, is going to be a big deal, as you call it in Boston. And he added as if an afterthought, "And Vinograd will finance it. Millions. Not pesetas, dollars."

He held up a warning hand but I hadn't planned to say anything. "He thinks we are working for him—but Otto Vinograd is making the biggest mistake of his life. Now I have to get on with my work. I'm talking too much. It's because I hate it when people underestimate me. Never mind. You're all right, I think. So. When you know where you're putting up, let us have the address."

I walked out with a nod. The first bench I came to, I sat down and inspected my pockets. My passport, the canceled American Express card, four unused metro tickets, the new five hundred francs from Miguel, a few French coins, a handkerchief, the used Bordeaux train ticket which I dropped on the ground, expired charter return flight, a ballpoint, a piece of paper with the Martel phone number. That, and my leaky shoes and green suit. Making this inventory calmed me down. With these worldly goods and nothing more I do myself endow.

I walked to the subway station and took the metro to the Val de Grace hospital. It was visiting hours when I got there, and I entered with a stream of people, carrying a bunch of flowers I bought at the entrance. I wandered down myriad corridors, for I thought it too risky to ask questions. Finally I discovered two policemen in that same kind of uniform I had seen once before, at the bridge. They were sitting on a bench in a corridor, talking in low voices. The door across from them had a No Entry sign hanging on the doorknob, and I sat down one bench further down the corridor with my flowers beside me.

People went in and out, but the door never opened wide until a man showed up with a gas cylinder on a trolley. When he had gone in, the door remained open for a moment, and I stood up. I saw the bed, the white face, unfrowning now but very old, twenty years older, and the mustache which I saw was more grey than red. The eyes were closed, the head bandaged. His bed cover rose just once as if he were sighing deeply. The mustache looked dead, it was out of place and as ridiculous as a theater mustache pasted onto a marble statue.

I stood there motionless until the door was shut by someone inside the room.

44

After the hospital, I went back to my fleabite hotel. Only when I was standing in my room and staring at that dirty wall outside my window (it looked more like the bottom of an old ship, I thought), did I focus on the fact that all my stuff had gone, and then, luckily before I had gone downstairs to scream at the hotel man, did I realize I had packed it myself and that my suitcase was still in St. Jean. No big loss, though. I kept seeing the chalk-white face with the greyish mustache on the striped hospital pillow and did not concentrate too well on my future moves. I hit the street again (as we don't say in Boston) but I stayed clear of the fast foods and purely by chance came upon a little restaurant where they had two long tables with wine in carafes on them and where everyone was more or less eating the same; I walked out with a lovely comfortable warmth of ragout and wine in my stomach. On the strength of it I just flopped out on my bed and slept like a child. My clothes were dirty but then the hotel linens were even dirtier, so that all balanced out.

Next day I found a message downstairs to call Miguel "immediately" and I dutifully descended to the basement of the neighboring café for greater privacy. They still had a tokens phone and it was a mistake to go there anyway because after a few moments a man came and posted himself outside the glass door, kept staring at me, and every now and again ticked on the door with his token. My waving him away and various other hand signals I tried on him were without effect. It was within that ambiance, if that's the word for standing next to a pissoir with its door wide open, that I had to settle my future and was more or less sent back home—to America that is.

"You read the morning paper," Miguel said. "He died."

Damnation. But literally. Think of those journeys, mine from Boston, Snail from Marseilles as I remember, and he from an office in a small French town, crossing in one point, in one instant.

"Now—" Miguel continued when he realized I had nothing to say, "Now—you stand out like a sore thumb here. Don't you think that you—" He waited a while. "We have room for Americans," he told me, "but in America."

"What *exactly* are you talking about, what do you want me to do? Fuck off! Fous le camp!" Those last bits were for the man outside the booth who looked ready to strangle me.

"We will work it all out. Go to this address. Write it down. 24 West 299th Street. The Bronx, I think. New York. You got that?"

"24 West 299th Street. I don't think there's such an address." I had to hold on to the door of the booth now, which the man tried to open.

"I'll be in touch," Miguel said.

"Miguel, wait! Is this serious? I lost my New York apartment. And how am I supposed to get there? I've got three hundred francs and that is all."

"Well, fuckit man, how had you ever planned to return?"

I said my return ticket had expired while we were in St. Jean. That was almost true.

I let go of the door and the man stumbled back; I came out and kicked him as hard as I could, in his balls maybe, in his belly anyway. He sort of yelped and ran back up the stairs. "Miguel!" I cried, "I just kicked a guy in his balls! I've never done a thing like that in my life. I'm changing. I'm becoming a Basque!"

"Did you hear what I said," Miguel said. "Will you fucking listen? Go to the Sophisticated Traveler Bureau, Rue Losserand, in the Quatorzième, tell 'em I sent you. And for the love of God, go. Go today." He hung up.

I opened a door marked "privé" and found myself in a very dirty kitchen. A boy was dragging a garbage can out into the alley and I followed him out.

It was a long flight. When they broke out the wines, I alternated between red and white. That had brought me luck at the Foreign Press Club. Well, luck. It had set me on my journey. My lonesome trail.

But now I was traveling under some kind of flag. Not solitary. When they brought out meal trays, I used the little knife to saw my American Express card into bits. No more of that stuff. There's some kind of sense to it all. Some kind. Some kind.

Someone made a short film once, it became famous, it was called "Incident at Battle Creek" or a name like that. About a man who is to be hanged as a spy during the American Civil War. The rope breaks and he escapes, you see him making his way home to his wife and when he puts his arms around her, his head snaps back and the hangman's rope kills him. The adventure of his escape was but a dream of the last minutes of his life.

I am writing this down because I know that my trek from Comillas to Frankfurt to Teresin, Strasbourg, Paris, and now back to New York may be such a dream. An awake dream, and when I am eye to eye with Maria, when perhaps I hold out my arm just to touch her hand, a doctor from the rest home comes in with his Valium injection, or maybe Vinograd with those two policemen from the TV photograph in Miguel's office ... But in this instant the plane is real, it is shaking slightly and the seatbelt lights will go on soon. Below me white clouds are spreading and the late sunlight is sharp enough to hurt my eyes. Such disparate and beautiful elements come from outside, my mind would not have the power to produce them.

Time is visible too. The watch on the wrist of the man across the aisle says 8:10. Quite a while ago it said 7:44. Where is my own watch? If I can remember that, I am sane. Did I pawn it? No. Leave it in the hospital in Teresin? No, they would have warned me. Did the Senegal journalist steal it too? No. I left it on Claire's night table in that flowermonth hotel. I see it quite clearly, half hidden by that large comb of hers.

He: upon his arrival he had money for the Carey bus to the New York eastside and just one dime more. He stood on that corner facing Grand Central station and tossed heads or tails with his dime and it slipped through his hands and vanished in the gutter. The immigration inspector had looked a long time at him, at his suit, and at every page in his passport.

It was getting dark. He wandered past the double-parked taxis and cars picking up passengers from the buses, and confronted the avenues. There was a roar of machines, a crew breaking open a trench. A murder in a doorway would remain unheard here, the cries of the victim issuing soundlessly from her mouth opening and closing. He started walking faster and faster, shops were closing, alarms were getting ready to howl. I haven't changed, I wasn't ready to come back, I'm still weak. Miguel took me by surprise.

He stopped at a telephone to dial Claire, and his apartment, but remembered he had no money. When he got to Central Park he sat on a bench for a while, and then trudged up Central Park West. On the wide steps of a building he ensconced himself in a corner. Warm air blew over him from somewhere. I mustn't fall asleep here, that wouldn't be very safe. For lack of a mirror, he took out his passport and studied his photograph. How funny and different I looked not very long ago, the girl who came with me to have those pictures taken told me to slick down my hair with water, you look like a hippie, she said. The photographer said to her, "He's very handsome." "Isn't he?" the girl smiled. Then he made her order too many prints.

He shook his head at the man in the photograph. Sacra simplicitas. He pulled the cover of the passport off and then tore the pages into pieces. From now on I am only Iberria.

When a flock of people started coming up the steps, he followed them in and found himself in a science museum. From a bench he watched two children play on the stone floor. They were dirty. They were eating from a plastic bag, quarreling, scattering candy wrappers and bits of food. Behind them, looming over them, three big men in space suits were staring out into endlessness with blind blue eyes. Little flags on their suits showed their right of arrogation, explorers who had planted their flags on themselves.

Above their heads, suspended from steel wires, hung a vast, pointed cylinder, space satellite or perhaps missile. It vibrated almost imperceptibly when below them the subway train rumbled by. The plastic bag, emptied by the children, stayed on the stone floor when they ran off, and moved slowly with the air currents in the hall. He had a vision of disasters and of a fatal flaw somewhere in this journey of his.

She: as Miguel had known, Maria had arrived in New York. The town remained not much more than a name to her: it was a meeting place. What she still liked to consider "the four elements": air, water, fire, and earth, were in New York as everywhere else.

In the fantasies of Lucas she was an emissary from the past, from the golden age when women reigned. Her very face confirmed for him that in that era the logic of history was feminine, and therefore benevolent. Then came the Battle of the Titans when the male idea won and aggression became the norm. Lucas is hard to take, maybe, and it is easy to dismiss all this. His muttering of Greek and Latin hexameters and pentameters doesn't help his case. For him she was the Greek moon goddess in disguise; he did not think of her as literally immortal, but he thought about "the immortality of beauty." That did not mean "forever" but for the span allotted to life on earth. Her existence on earth, the existence of such perfection, affirmed that justice was possible here.

Surely such ideas have as much reality as what is routinely accepted as our fate, our tasks, our reason for being alive.

But however that may be, Maria was lying low (as she called it herself). Very few New Yorkers laid eyes on her, a few waiters and cab drivers perhaps and the odd passer-by as she slipped from a car into an entrance. Possibly they were aware of something unusual about her, but New York has plenty of beautiful women.

It was about dinner time when I got to my old apartment. No one in sight and on my mailbox Jos had inserted a piece of cardboard with his name over mine. I rang bells until someone buzzed the door open and I climbed up to my old door, locked of course. But I had always kept a spare key behind the hot water pipes in the closet next to it and it was still there. At least Jos hadn't changed the lock. Here I stood on a seagreen Chinese mat and did not even recognize the place, Jos who had claimed he hadn't the money to send me two months' rent and who in fact had not sent anything, had redecorated with carpets and color stripes and, hard to believe, trompes l'oeil as in the *New York Times* Living Section about famous people in small apartments. I took a long shower and put some of Jos' underwear on as all my own stuff seemed to have vanished. I sat down to wait.

It was nine o'clock when he came in with a girl, and before I could start swearing at him, he was swearing at me. Yes, he had wired the rent and a deal was a deal.

"I don't believe you," I said.

"This guy is really something," the girl informed Jos.

"I can tell you two met in a bookstore," I told him. "Your friend has a way with words."

I asked him for next month's rent and he asked me, had I paid it, there had been a bill and a nasty letter in the mail. He had an argument there.

We settled on his lending me twenty dollars and my sleeping a night or two on the couch, a nasty thing about five feet long. Which was all for the best, as it was a sure-fire encouragement not to hang around but to go see what was going on at Miguel's West 299th Street address.

I reached it a late afternoon, quite a walk beyond the last subway station; it was a seedy neighborhood all right but in my green suit, now a more slimy green, I fitted in fine. The door was opened by an unshaven fat man in a T-shirt who looked like a beery super but who later turned out to be a twice exiled Basque former actor, first exiled from Spain and then from Chile. His name was Salvador.

"Are you the Frenchman from Miguel?" Salvador asked me.

"I come from Miguel but I'm an American."

"But you have an accent?"

"No."

"Good. Very good. We need someone like that." Then he had given me a room. He also lent me an old but clean bathrobe and I put everything I had on in the washing machine. We had a beer and a pizza which he had ordered by phone, and then I went to sleep in a big, real, bed. For that first meeting I had adopted a policy of not asking any questions, which came natural to me; the whole atmosphere in the place was a bit of wartime resistance fighters hiding from the Germans as you see in late night movies, and in fact I heard later that they called that place "the safehouse" (as if it were one word). I realize resistance fighters didn't order pizza by telephone. Salvador had asked me if I was ready to help him the following day on "a project," and I had said yes.

A picture taken of the waterfront at the end of the street would have looked nice enough. Sea, a road skirting a beach, a tree or two. But stepping back you'd have seen the more usual way in which land and water meet these days: debris, empty shacks, winter skeletons of hot-dog stands and vandalized Coke machines, the whole seamed with a line of worn-out cars. All this not far from the safehouse, and where the Bronx met the ocean or maybe the Sound.

A mile away, beyond, a stone wall, large houses looked out on the same water hiding the same sewage. Or perhaps not, perhaps the wall continued under the sea right around the globe. Here on this side lived those who did not even have the shoreline tan they could have had for free; their faces were pale, even glaucous, if tinted maybe by the genes of a long perished African or Indian parent. They carried loud radios or wore walkmans to obliterate the here and now and owned lumbering cars to leave in to nowhere. It was here that Salvador took me to a storefront where there was nothing but a trestle table covered with cardboard boxes and a couple of kitchen chairs.

"Jesus, what do we want with this mess?"

"Mess? You'll be surprised," Salvador said with a coy smile. It was hard to think of this man with a week of black stubble on his boxer's face as coy, but it was definitely a coy smile he produced. He turned over an army carryall he had brought and shook it out on the table. A pile of stuffed envelopes came out, a cardboard sign, and also a thermos and paper cups. He poured us two vile coffees. "This area was marked for gentrification," he told me, "ten city blocks. The landlords walked away from it, that is two years ago, and then nothing happened. Now we're going to gentrify it, not the buildings but the people. In those boxes are the forms, the envelopes have money. You can't hand out money without forms, people don't trust you, right?"

"Yes. I guess so."

"Listen, friend," Salvador said, "You're not interested but you're wrong. This is not a big deal, convenido, but it's a start. It's our first project. You will see. This shop belongs to a Basque family, a Basque refugee family. Everything is interconnected."

"So what's UNAC stand for?" That is what it said on the sign.

He looked at it as if he hadn't seen it before, and then propped it up in the window. "You'll see," he repeated.

The door opened and a man in a T-shirt came in, with tattooed forearms and a bewildered, child-like, expression on his face. "What's this all about then?" he asked. "Menolo said, go there."

Salvador beamed at him. "We're the new rehabilitation center. Sit down, won't you, and fill out this form."

"I don't know about this," the man said, staring at it.

"Just leave open what you don't want to answer. Here," and Salvador handed him one of the sealed envelopes.

The man put it in his pocket without opening it. "Just spread the word," Salvador told him. "That's all we ask."

When the door had closed on the man, Salvador looked at me and rubbed his hands. "Can you see his face when he opens that envelope?"

"Yeah. It's great. What's in it?"

"They're all different." He peered at me. "Nothing less than a thousand dollars."

"No kidding! Who's paying for all this?"

"Ah. That would be telling."

I shrugged.

He didn't like my indifference. "Dr. Otto Vinograd," he said almost triumphantly.

I frowned at him. How did I get stuck with these nuts?

"You don't believe me. It's complex. It's a first payment, and then again, it's like a bribe. Vinograd wants to move his headquarters to Bilbao. Bilbao in an autonomous Euzkadi. They've promised him complete freedom of movement. Now do you believe me."

"Miguel told me, Vinograd was his enemy," I said.

"Oh he is, he is. He thinks he's tricking us, but we're the ones who are tricking him. But he is very rich and powerful, this man. We are careful. He has the biggest private house in New York City, did you know that? On Fifth Avenue and 73rd Street. I've seen it."

"With computers in every bedroom, right?"

"What? I don't know. I wasn't inside."

Four or five people had come in and they were waiting patiently until Salvador stopped talking. Then one came up and said, "Tommy told us—"

"Yes, sure," Salvador told him, beaming again. "Sit down. Fill this out. Here's a pen."

49

An hour later, there was a line outside to the corner. It was oddly quiet, I think people were afraid any hassle or commotion could spoil the whole thing. But they didn't look happy as they came into the storefront, the mood in there had become uneasy no matter how hard Salvador smiled and shook hands. Just before twelve a man showed up who identified himself as from the mayor's office. Salvador told me to deal with him. "This is where you come in," he whispered, "I haven't even got a Green Card."

I took the man into the little backroom and told him we were working for a foundation, giving interest-free loans to the Third World.

"And the Bronx is the Third World?" he asked.

"Sure. Why not. Como no. We're testing it out."

"And what does UNAC stand for?"

"We have United Nations observer status."

"Can you show me identification as a recognized charity?"

"This isn't a charity! These are ex-gratia payments."

"Oh. Eh—but do you have a city license to do this?"

"A license, for paying out money?"

"I'll go and consult my superior," he said. He hesitated at the back door. "You people better watch your step, you're getting in the way of a lot of enterprise around here—with all that sudden money, how they're going to find girls—" He did not finish the sentence.

Who could have thought that handing out dollars could make you feel so unpleasant? "I'm not surprised," Salvador said when I sat back down beside him. He had run out of steam too. "This isn't an antidote to misery, it's misery in reverse."

Before long our unease was taken care of. Two men made their way to the front of the line and one of them opened his raincoat and showed us he was holding a sawn-off shotgun underneath it. A minute later they had driven off with the remaining envelopes; no one had said a word. A police car which had politely waited, double-parked, until they had pulled away, took their place and the same city official reappeared, this time with a police lieutenant in tow.

"You just missed it," I told them with a certain glee. "We're closed up."

"Stealing money is more fun than handing it out," Salvador said that evening. "In Chile, after the coup, when we needed money to get out of the country, we broke into a Loan Company office. I got stuck in the window. We had a good time."

We were sitting in silence for hours. Or maybe I simply hadn't been listening to him. He stood up and said, "I wasn't alone then."

"When?"

"When I was stuck in the window of the loan company."

He struck a strange pose, he looked as a musician with a cup does, watching you as you pass him on a subway platform. (It was much later that he told me he was a stage actor by profession.) He said, "In solitude things are born and die, and reason grows and grows until it is madness. La razón crece y crece hasta ser desvarío. That is Pablo Neruda."

"That is me too," I said but not loud enough for him to hear. But later I asked him to write down the Spanish for me.

50

We were told to lie low for a number of days. Salvador passed the word on to me. I stayed indoors although the chance that someone I knew in New York would pass by all the way up here and see me was nil. Salvador offered me a choice from various articles of clothing in the closets, but I stayed with my green suit. I sat by myself mostly, a paperback found here or there in my lap, the old television set with its ugly greenish screen turned toward the wall, and I watched the boys in the street selling their little screwed-up pieces of paper with

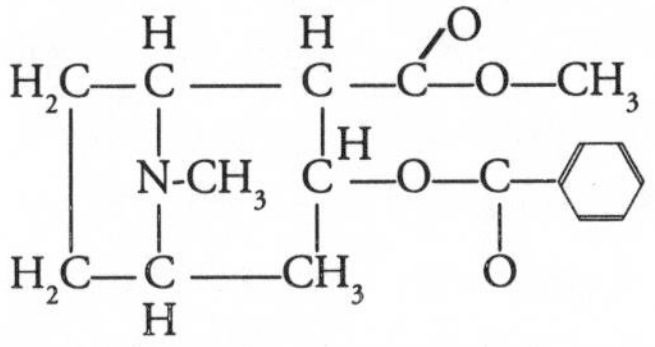

```
        H        H    /O
H2C—C ——— C —C—O—CH3
  |     |      |H
  |   N-CH3  C —O—C—⬡
  |     |      |      |
H2C—C ———CH3        O
        H
```

$C_{17}H_{21}NO_4$, that malignant combination of atoms themselves as clean as water, earth, and air once were, benzoylmethyl ecgonine, cocaine.

E pluribus unum. An exact image of the children (that is what they were), each of them by himself innocently destined to a natural life and a natural death, but come together in a malignant structure that would leave them, and many more, dead. They lay rotting, killed in the night, on the sidewalks, or gutted, packed still half-alive in plastic bags and thrown into the trunks of old automobiles driving off in a roar of defunct transmissions and oil smoke.

Meanwhile their once girlfriends, girls who for a brief year had sat next to them in school and had had their hairs pulled and made fun of and later had been kissed and caressed and, maybe, loved, were selling the use of their sore and infected cunts on the corners of this same street to pay for—for what? An extension of lives already ended. Why this all happened in this way I cannot know, no visible purpose was served, not even the most perverse one, no law or lawlessness of nature obeyed. "The market forces," Salvador said. "A couple of men here and in my part of the world below the Rio Bravo get very very rich from this."

"From that boy across the street whose bowels are hanging out where he was cut up? He looks fourteen."

"Where?" He rushed to the window. "There's no one there."

"You're too late. Or too early. He will be there, what is the difference."

Salvador looked up and down the street and shook his head.

"Our next distributions should be in Columbia or Mexico or some such place," I said. "In those devastated countrysides."

"They should. In fact, it is being considered."

They did decide just that. I have little Spanish and would be of no use in such an operation, but he insisted I come along and even went to the trouble of getting me a new, doctored passport.

We did not set up shop in the countryside though. We would have been too visible, an irritation to men whose interests lay elsewhere. We housed our office in a popular city church, a huge and atrociously ugly building of turrets and excrescences run by a mild man who called himself a working priest. Actually he was the bishop. An obscure charity was brought in under whose banner we could function. No one bothered to change the UNAC on the form and indeed, it could stand for whatever you wanted.

We were hasty this time, for we were nervous; but at the other side of the desks no unease existed. Cash payments, handouts, were more within a local tradition here. Our customers were solemn rather than subdued.

Midmorning of the first day, protesters were dropped off from an open truck in front of the church. They carried signs, "NO to Gringo charity." Then a van appeared from a local television station and they wanted to know who was organizing this. Salvador talked to them. I missed much of what was said. The interviewer, with his blow-dried hair and hostile jollity, was just like most of his colleagues up north.

Soon various other men pulled up in their cars, and finally our bishop reappeared in the sacristy. Consultations in low voices followed and it ended with the bishop telling us we'd better stop with what we were doing, there were ramifications here he had not been aware of.

Salvador had been muttering a simultaneous translation in my ear the way they do it at the United Nations electronically—more as a joke than because it seemed useful to him—and I could see on the bishop's face that he agreed with whomever had told him to put an end to it. He himself shooed out the indignant men and women who had been waiting in line, and I heard him use the word "pecado" a couple of times. Pecado means sin: I assume he told them it would be a sin to accept our money. And maybe it was.

51

But we had our pride too. Salvador went to see his local contact or maybe contacts and they decided, no more hiding behind others, we were going to take this money directly to the people in one of the misery towns, villas miserias as they called them. A nice looking van was rented for the next morning and Salvador's local friend José turned up with two men in uniform for an escort. They were actually army recruits on sick leave but they looked as bloody-minded as any security guard. Off we were, into the countryside this time.

A melancholy bit of countryside it was, dry, eroded, fields with a goat here and there trying to remember what grass looks like, and garbage dumps where kids were competing for the scraps with seagulls who had the advantage because the smells didn't seem to bother them. Or maybe seagulls have no sense of smell. At times a factory vomiting sulphur and soot but at least feeding some people while it lasted.

We heard music from somewhere off the road, and we both began to shout, "Make for it, José!" He was driving.

Surprise, we hit upon a fairground, a shabby fairground but a fairground. The merry-go-round was pushed by a man and a child, the Big Wheel was driven by a steam engine stoked with wood and about to collapse, there was the woman with the beard, and a blind dog pulling lottery tickets out of a straw screen. And over it all the very mighty music of a paso doble was wafted to the visitors from the villa miseria which ended right at the edge of the fairground.

Salvador climbed out and went to talk to the owner of the blind dog. Then he told José to pull up behind the lottery stand. The van got stuck in the mud and we had to push him there.

"This will be sweet," Salvador said to me. He had these gentle words in English—or maybe he used the same in Spanish.

He had fixed it that the man with the dog would hand out the envelopes full of pesos. The dog pulled out tickets and each ticket was a winner. Pretty soon everyone came to line up at that stand and once children started running home with the news, the whole villa miseria emptied out. But this time no hassles, no one was suspicious, it went like a dream. "Ninguno dos veces!" Salvador, standing on an oil drum, cried, "no one twice." But even if someone went twice, so what?

Then the latecomers from the villa miseria began trickling in. They made up the rear because they came hobbling on crutches and wooden legs, a parade as out of a Brueghel painting. But our century went him one better, because at least half of them were children. A little girl on one leg had crutches made out of pieces of a wooden pole, a legless boy pushed himself in a crate on wheels. A woman standing beside me saw my agitation; "Minas," she muttered, landmines.

Salvador, on his oil drum, had to bend down constantly to receive the kisses that came his way. The merry-go-round man produced rum to toast us, and the poor blind dog got into such frenzy that he kept running to and fro when there was nothing left to pick and that he tore the straw screen to shreds. And finally we got back aboard our van and started backing out of the mud, and the villa miseria people put their gramophone on a flatbed truck and drove by our side all the way to the big road, serenading us with their paso doble, which seemed to be the only record they had. If a car had come from the other direction, we would all have ended up in a musical crash, but it didn't.

52

I was standing on First Avenue, facing the United Nations building. I combed my hair in the black glass of an office window to make myself more respectable. Then I crossed the street and went into the secretariat. I had come to see Maria Farari. The guards weren't too enchanted with the way I looked, but eventually one of them phoned the public information people, and a halfway helpful man came down to see me.

What was I about? After our fairground adventure we were all on a high, and José took us to a cantina where we drank beers and rums and beers with rum poured in them. I talked with José, as well as we could with my lousy Spanish and his less lousy English, and I told him something of my pursuit. Salvador, with his past as a Basque militant and all, wasn't a man I could ever have talked to that way, he was too political, too suspicious. José was vague, very cheerful, and he knew all about Jason and the Golden Fleece, moreover. Just before we broke up the party, he whispered to me, "I know her, the woman you are searching for. You can meet her. She tries to help political prisoners and the disappeared of our countries, los desaparecidos. You will find her at the U.N. mostly. Her name is Maria Farari."

Could it be that simple? I did not know whether to believe this, I think I was afraid to find it true. But here I was. I told the public info man that I had come to the U.S. to see Maria Farari, and after some to's and fro's he became friendly. He went to the reception desk and made two phone calls. Then he asked me to come back at two o'clock. It had just turned ten.

Those were long hours to spend in one, then another, First Avenue coffee shop. I went to the toilet a couple of times, mostly to look at myself in the mirror. Seeing my pale bewildered face with its red-rimmed eyes, it appeared highly doubtful to me that someone with a face like that could have a role to play, a role in history.

It's hard for me to understand that so many men in history were able to scrutinize their own faces, their bloodshot eyes, their weak mouths (maybe hidden under little fancy beards) and then walk out into a day of ordering hundreds of prisoners to be shot, hundreds or thousands of soldiers to run up against machine guns.

At half past one I crossed back over to the UN. I stood around in the lobby and when my man came back from lunch, he made me wait in a little windowless room on the third floor where I read xeroxed announcements about the Christmas Savings Club and a scheduled hike on Staten Island. I tried closing my eyes and thinking back to the start of it all, which usually gives me new strength, but my head remained stubbornly empty. It was much later when the man reappeared. I think he looked disappointed that I hadn't given up and left. "Please follow me," he said.

I trailed him through one corridor after another until I thought I couldn't possibly still be in the same building. He stopped in front of a door and I expected some excuse for sending me off, but he opened the door and motioned me to go in.

An office in beige and brown colors, with the low sun lighting up everything to the farthest corners. I walked toward the desk, where a woman was standing with her back toward the light, and looking past her I saw the dry fountain of the UN forecourt.

"I am Maria Farari," she said. "And you are—?"

My heart beat very fast when I turned my eyes toward her. A friendly smile lit her sad face, face of one of the Buenos Aires mothers who had held up photographs of their murdered children to the backs of colonels getting in and out of limousines across the street from them. I swallowed. "A misunderstanding," I muttered, "forgive me," and I almost ran from the room.

53

I made my way up First Avenue, shaken by the unforgivable manner I had walked out of her room, without even looking at her; I had made her invisible as so many times before in her life men had made her invisible to them.

At 49th Street the traffic was at a standstill. I crossed from my side, already in the freezing twilight, to the last sun on the other sidewalk. There was a lot of glass on the ground and a revolving red beam began sweeping through it like a lighthouse gone mad, and made the shards light up like rubies. I looked back and saw a police car sitting on the sidewalk, and then two cops standing in my path. "We're taking you in," one of them said in a neutral tone of voice.

"For what?"

"We don't like your suit."

In the police station I was one in a whole line, all men my age more or less, all white. There were fingerprints and mug shots. Others arrested there showed driver's licenses or credit cards but I had nothing to show. I was who I thought I was. A sergeant read me some stuff, and then told me, "You're held on a charge of aiding and abetting in the kidnaping of a Doctor Winegrad from Germany."

"You are joking," I answered.

"We're short of space," those were the only other words addressed to me as I was put in a day cell holding a mixed bag of what looked like pushers and pimps and maybe a couple of Winegrad kidnapers, and even women, whores, apathetically sitting around. Its toilet had cut-up newspapers but it was a tough place, you could tell (prison johns I've known never had paper).

A man approached me as I was pacing up and down muttering, and said, "Hey, you, you're in a hurry to get out, am I right, you do me a favor and I'll have you bailed today. Leave it to me."

Time passed.

I was sitting on the floor, blowing on one of the half-frozen bologna sandwiches they had passed out (most prisoners had thrown theirs on a pile of them in a corner, but I'm not proud), when I saw blood on my hand. A trickle of blood and slime was running along the floor past my legs. Crouched in a corner, not even lying down, crouched like a stone-age woman in front of her little fire, one of the whores was giving birth. She was screaming, but as an alarm somewhere outside was going without pause, you could only see this, not hear it. I tried to get to my feet but was held down: the same man who had accosted me earlier was leaning on my shoulders with both hands.

"Stay out of it, fellow," he shouted over the noise. "They wanna fuck, they take the consequences. I need you outside." Other inmates started banging on the bars, screaming, "Get that bitch out of here!" and stuff like that. At long last two uniformed women appeared, handcuffed the whore, threw a towel over her belly, and dragged her away. My cellmates applauded. The moment the cell door banged behind her, the alarm stopped.

They did let me out as the man had promised but I now carried a piece of paper with an address where I was to pick up something for him. That man had a face which made it impossible for me not to stick to the deal. When I got to the place, they gave me a manila envelope to take across town, with ten dollars for a taxi. So far so good, but at the other end there was another envelope waiting, a jiffy bag to be taken to Riverdale. "Your man said, one errand," I objected, and got a slap in my face. "Just do it," they said. "Take a Liberty bus. Taxis can be traced."

When I got off that bus it was night, there was a police car at the bus stop, they told me to get in, and beat me up. We've read those words, someone being beaten up in the back of a police car but the reality feels different from what the words conjure up. There is so little room there, what hurts most is the door handles, the wire netting in front of the seat.

The two men in the police car, cops or pushers, thugs or undercover feds, who knows, knocked him unconscious and took the jiffy bag away from under his clothes. They drove downtown afterward and left him on a bench in Central Park near the East 65th Street exit. It was no particular luck that they did not kill him, they had no reason and thus didn't bother to.

Lucas came to soon thereafter but he couldn't move his arms or legs yet. He lay there, looking up at the night sky, wondering. A hole in the road next to his bench still held water from the rain and sleet that had fallen that day and in it a star was reflected. Instead of considering his state, he kept opening and closing one eye or the other, watching the star shift in its bit of water.

A gigantic globe of burning hydrogen far out in a void was reflecting itself in a puddle of rain water, a straight line of light connected those two over a distance of a thousand light years. Hold on to that image, try to think yourself away by your grasp of it.

He saw that his left hand was bleeding freely. Painfully he lowered himself to the ground and moved the hand under the surface of the water, letting his blood darken the puddle.

54

Vinograd's house, not the Frankfurt Schloss but his pied-à-terre on Fifth Avenue, stood out lightlessly among its lesser neighbors. Snow had started falling on Central Park and I had hobbled over from my bench, eight slow and painful blocks. Vinograd and his police buddies. The snow was coming down in concentric circles now with me in the middle, at a side door, ringing a bell. I hadn't thought out what precisely I was going to do there but now that this enormous place indeed seemed to stand empty and unguarded, my apprehensions vanished, only anger was left.

The door remained locked and I gave it a kick which reverberated up my spine. I looked east and west but there wasn't a soul on the street, it was past midnight. I gave another mighty kick, making so much noise that I hastened around the corner. Silence. I went back and found the door ajar. No alarms, but I saw a red string with a blob of wax swinging from a jamb; I had broken a police seal. I got my bruised body in out of the cold.

Dim light shining into the corridor led me to a kind of porter's lodge where a wall cabinet was filled with jars of instant coffee and packages of cream crackers. I ate some, they were wet and soft, but the coffee which I made with warm tapwater was all right. After this supper I went back out into the corridor and listened for sounds. There were none.

I came out into the front lobby behind a monumental door which was, idiotically, barred with a whole set of bolts and locks. The only light came from small dials on metal boxes—alarm systems? The air vibrated with the unending low hum which now takes the place of silence. When my eyes had become adjusted to the semidarkness, I started my second walk through a Vinograd house, in an attempt perhaps to repeat the first one that had led to the photograph of the dead Mrs. Vinograd and the newspaper clipping of another photograph, hers, Maria's.

I did not find his bedroom this time. I did find a room with a Bayeux Invasion tapestry of tanks and guns exactly like the Frankfurt one; I touched it and found it wasn't a tapestry but printed, smooth, paper. Once you looked close, you saw that it shimmered in the minimal light, very different from cloth; it made it the more threatening. Wallpaper designed for a command post from which to oversee the burning of England, or the razing of Moscow.

Unlike my first house call on Vinograd, this time I did not calm down, I became increasingly fearful, going ever faster through the dark and cold rooms, superstitiously touching vases and paintings in passing, tempting alarms to go off. I saw now that *everything* was a facsimile, undegradable plastic etched with lasers or something to get the color and texture of real materials—everything being like something else. I sat down and asked myself why he had repeated his Frankfurt Schloss this way. I realized, no, I saw that vases and tapestries and paintings weren't copies of the Frankfurt ones, they were the selfsame.

I started up and down staircases and wandered down corridors. I found an inlaid table which on the touch of a button unveiled a cabinet of liqueurs, green and pink bottles with twigs, grasses, and whole fruits swimming in them. I sat on the floor then and drank from them all. A warm glow thawed out my beat-up cold limbs. And then I came upon a huge bathroom, built in black and white marble. The tub itself had steps leading into it. Above it a vast silver mirror was set in the ceiling.

It was quite light in there for the sky had cleared and moonlight flooded in through a clerestory of windows. I took off my filthy clothes and opened the enormous taps. Then I floated within that marble shell and my pains and frustrations and helpless angers all drew out of me.

I looked up in the mirror above me and saw myself in the whitish water as if I was up there too, part of a Tiepolo ceiling, and a sudden wave of lust swept over me. I saw my own body for the first time since Comillas.

I could see my erection and I came the second I touched it. The orgasm wasn't enough to change my mood, I went on stroking myself. The white semen in the water didn't disgust me, I went on. A solitary orgy.

I dried myself and went back naked to the Bayeux tapestry room. I stood in front of it, drinking from one of the bottles of liqueur. I stroked myself with one hand and grabbed the pseudo tapestry with the other, and it came off the wall with a great tearing sound. It fell around my feet in a smooth and slippery pile, caressing me, and I came again. Then I vomited up those horrible sweetish alcohols. I was shivering now, I wiped myself with the towel, wrapped it around me and sat down at a little desk. I bent the desk lamp down low, so its light would not reach a window, and turned it on.

I grabbed books from the wall beside me and put them down under the lamp. They all had leather covers stamped with gold, but they weren't books at all, they were blocks of wood to which sixteenth and seventeenth century book covers had been glued. Inside the cover of the first one I opened was a label, which read, "RM Cave 1 Gannett, 3, HFD 24.40." The others were all similar. Wood disguised as books, wooden blocks on wooden shelves. In some of the oldest, on the top shelf, which I now took down, the labels were handwritten. One said, "Original in Rocky Mountains Cave 1, level 3."

Vinograd not only collected facsimiles, he held the originals and had hidden them.

I knew that some libraries did this or perhaps still do. The New York 42nd Street Library had rare books sent to caves and disused mines in the fifties, and put wooden blocks in their place; I had seen them in the Rare Book Room. Did it mean that Vinograd saw himself as a conservator of civilization? Or were he and perhaps other men buying and hiding everything real we have in order to survive with that reality in deep caves of their own? Were the rest of us already living in a counterfeit world?

I opened a box on a shelf and found it held racks of transparencies. I held one up against the light of the desk lamp. It was a diapositive of a painting I had never seen before. The slides were all of old paintings, but there were no numbers or letters on them or on their containers. I picked some others out at random: one I recognized as a Watteau I had seen in a museum. I went over to a Greek vase with naked satyrs and pushed it off its pedestal, and it did not break but rolled away with a hollow sound.

I had to throw up again. I was very cold and vainly tried to find a rug or anything woven to cover myself better. There was nothing but the coils of gleaming paper on the floor, piles of color slides, plastic vases, toy soldiers.

I set out to find the bathroom back where my clothes were. I left the underwear and got back in the green suit. I had some bad moments trying to find that monumental door leading to the porter's lodge. And then I was out on the street as empty as before, with the snow falling again in fat, pure, flakes.

55

A bloomin' miracle, the change from those drug guys' money for the Liberty bus was still in the pocket of my jacket. I took a subway and a bus, and when I banged on the door of our so-called safehouse it was just getting light.

"What the hell," Salvador said when he had finally appeared in his flamboyant bathrobe, but when he saw my scratched black and blue face he shut up, led me inside and put me in the old easy chair facing the TV. "Sit," he said. "I'm making coffee." I closed my eyes and the night receded. Salvador was concerned, he brought his (terrible) coffee and then he announced he was going to make eggs and toast, but he never asked me what had happened. I guess that was part of their code, but I had to tell someone something. "I was sent to see a Maria at the United Nations," I told him, "the wrong Maria. But they must be watching her or something, for when I came out, I got picked up by the cops. They were arresting people all over the place. And you know what for? Vinograd, Vinograd has been kidnaped. That's what they said. No such thing, I would guess."

"No such thing, compañero. Who sent you to the UN? José, I bet. He's a sweet guy, but he's an asshole. They're all a bunch of assholes."

What's going on, I was about to ask. But I didn't. What the hell. I just have to see Maria's face, just one more time, maybe. I want no part of all these shenanigans. "I have to get some sleep now," I told him.

He hesitated. "Vinograd is now in the country," he said. "If you must know, what's happening is, he's set up a phony kidnaping, getting kidnaped by ETA, the Basques, you know, with a forty million dollar ransom, he's insured for that, and we'll share the money. Or so it is planned."

"Ah. Well, I'd say, don't trust him. I'm sure he'll out-trick you all."

"Too right."

He still seemed to be waiting, waiting for something. "You didn't give my room to someone else, did you?" I asked, suddenly sure that was the explanation.

"No, of course not! What do you think. The thing is, they asked for you yesterday. But you weren't there of course."

"Who are 'they'? Asked to do what?"

"I don't know, do I? But it involved quite a trip."

"Is it too late now?"

"Well, you're not in shape for any long trips, are you?"

"I'm in fine shape. Come on, can't you phone somebody?"

He hesitated. "I guess—all right. You wait in the kitchen."

I could hear him shout in Spanish through the two walls. When he came back his face was red, and he nodded at me. "You're on. Here's the address. Go stand in Fordham Road, that's where lots of taxis go by at this time of the morning. You've got to go out of town. A hundred miles out of town. I haven't any money right now, you must tell the guy he'll get paid at the other end."

"No one's going to buy that. Here at 299 Street, the Bronx?"

"Just be convincing. Maybe you better shave first. I got some very soothing cream, it'll cool your face."

"Cool my face. You people are planning forty million dollar stunts and you haven't got the money for a taxi?"

He grinned. "That's how it goes in these affairs, compañero. Shall I tell you something? On January 1, 1947, they were all set to overthrow Franco. You know what went wrong? The phone hadn't been paid. No money. And on New Year's Day, January 1, a holiday of church and state, the fucking Madrid telephone company cut off their phones."

As I was shaving with his soothing cream, he came standing beside me. "I'll read you a clipping," he said. "From the *Figaro,* a Paris newspaper. I'll translate. Here goes. 'Cowardly attacked in a terrorist ambush, this

French customs officer has succumbed from head wounds. Here was a man who had served at our southern outpost of Hendaye for many years—a dramatic post in the history of France. Before his father—Before him, his father had served at that post for more than thirty years. A family of tradition—No union malcontents. In the tragic days of the summer of 1940, his father kept his post when so many politicians abandoned theirs. He was justified in his belief that his son would carry on in the tradition'—etcetera etcetera."

In an odd way this gave me new courage. The white face in the hospital bed had merged with the face fleetingly seen in the arc light of a border post, the face of the man saluting Vinograd's Mercedes. I know that was but a dream. That word, though, the word "but" has to be qualified. A dream has its reasons. There are links, links of blood. The path I am following, you may say, is an intuitive one; but "intuition" is but a label for a kind of reality we do not understand.

56

I stand in the road and one taxi after another stops for me because it is a sunny morning, but when they hear where I want to go, they look me over and ask for fifty dollars up front. I tell them they'll be paid at the other end but they drive off. After a long, long time, for all I know the next day, a black man with short grey hair says, okay, but it better be there, and we are on our way. He is eating a peanut-butter sandwich by the time we cross the George Washington Bridge and when he sees in his mirror the way I am looking at him, he breaks off half and gives it to me through the money chute.

"Things are tough, are they?" he asks.

"No—I'm finding my way."

"Good," he says.

The task they have for me at the other end of a hundred dollar taxi ride consists of "being in attendance on someone."

"Why me? In what way? As a guard?"

"A bit of everything. You'll be paid too. Take a beer."

After dark, an old man with an accent so heavy that I only understand a bit of what he mumbles, drives me in a VW bus. We go through empty countryside, mile after mile without a lighted window. I did not know there was so much wildness left in New York or New Jersey or wherever we are. We end up at a narrow brick house within a barbed wire fence with a man on guard. We walk silently from the bus to the house in a glacial wind under a sky full of angry purple clouds and too much light in it. I fail to understand the source of the light.

Two men are watching a Spanish station on TV and drinking coffee. They have arms, nothing fancy, what looks to me like World War Two Lee Enfield rifles, propped up against the backs of their chairs. They tell me I've been assigned to attend to the doctor, you know, Binograt.

"Vinograd?"

"Yes."

"No way."

The old man who drove me has put himself in front of the TV. But one of those two guards or whatever they are tells him, "Come on, pop, let's go. I want to get home." They leave. The rifles stay where they are.

"Let's sit down," the remaining man says. "Let me pour you some coffee."

He turns off the TV. "This is a very subtle business," he tells me. "The doctor, he asked specially for you."

"Impossible."

"But I'm telling you. The doctor is in retreat, I mean, having his retreat. That's what he has this house for. No one knows about it. I think it's medical, nothing to do with the Church. A doctor, I mean a real disease doctor, comes twice a day. No priests, nothing."

"Where do you all come in, anyway? Or Maria? Or for God's sake, me? I?"

"You don't know anything?" he asks.

"No."

"Drink your coffee, compadre."

"No."

"You don't like it?"

"No. Can I have a beer, and a sandwich?"

"But sure." He stands up and starts messing around with various hampers. "Now then. Don't say no before you've heard me out. Binograt in retreat, right? We here to protect him from any outsiders, right? But also, maybe, to make sure he won't be off before we're ready for that. All clear so far?"

I just make a face and he continues. "He's been sleeping badly. One guy he trusts, sort of a confidence man, you see, 'my private secretary' he calls, him, but this guy is sick and won't come. He *says*. I think, he's just worried, he wants to stay out of it."

"So do I."

"Wait. So yesterday he says, bring me that phony American journalist. At least he speaks English properly. I want to see him. So we ask Maria and she says, yes, okay, a good idea. We have to keep him happy, you see. We need the time. He got so much money, that Binograt. We are handing him with kid gloves."

"Handling."

"Okay, handling. We'll all end up being friends, you see. Como no. No shooting. Shaking hands. Adios."

"I can tell you one thing," I answer. "He'll eat you alive, our Dr. Vinograd will."

"But you'll see him?"

"I guess so. Since Maria wants it so. Where, when?"

"After dinner, he says. He wanted you yesterday, you know. In his retreat. You'll see. You'll be surprised."

When he has had a good look at me, he brings out various items, pants, a windbreaker, boots. I take the boots but I stay in my green suit for good luck.

I feel now like someone in one of those fairy tales when you have to pass three tests, like first the dog with the saucer eyes, then the dog with the soup plate eyes, then the dog with the millstone eyes, that sort of thing.

"What did I tell you?" the guard asked. "Surprising, no?" Behind the narrow brick house we had crossed a dense growth of trees, and now found ourselves in front of a small chateau, nothing less. Inside it was more like a Schloss again, with skins and heads of animals all over the walls, something like Mayerling in the Charles Boyer movie. The guard knocked on a curtained door and we came into a large room where there was only one little light in a corner; beside it a man was sitting up in a canopied bed. The guard steered me to a chair at the opposite end of the room and left.

Silence. My eyes adjusted to the twilight. A sharp voice, "Do you play blind chess?" I recognized the voice of Vinograd.

"No. I play regular chess."

"My eyes hurt, I want the room to stay darkened."

No sound but the hum from a machine behind the wall. The momentary racket of a passing helicopter.

"All this darkness," I muttered. "Not very good security for you, mine Herr."

He had heard. "There are infrared searchlights everywhere," he said. "Why, are you concerned for my welfare?"

"No, for my own perhaps."

"Ah yes, I am a murderer. I almost forgot. That is what makes me interested in you, the only thing, you can be sure. That portrait of my late wife you tossed on the table like the ace of spades. Tell me about it."

"Why should I? You may ask the police."

I could see him shrug. "Don't or do. I don't worry, rest assured. I am invulnerable in all my actions. I'll pay you for a good story, however."

"I was in Comillas at the same time as you," I told him. I had hoped to see some kind of reaction from him, but there wasn't any.

"And?" he asked.

I didn't answer.

"That's it? Sorry, no, with the best will I can't call that a good story. And here I had already written you a check for fifty thousand dollar." He waved a piece of paper. "My secretary decided to get ill just when I went into my yearly retreat. For my bodily health only, I assure you. My mind, my soul, are fine. The servants here are a flock or a herd, something from the animal world anyway, with a babel of uncouth dialects at their disposal. You speak English at least. So explain to me about my wife's portrait, and when you're at it, about why you seem to be around all the time. Entertain me fifty thousand dollars' worth." He lit a little cigar and I saw his face clearly for an instant. He wasn't looking at me.

"Did you learn about the Titans in your Frankfurt Gymnasium?" I asked with as much contempt in my voice as I could muster.

"I was born in Schaffhausen and attended the Gymnasium in Ingolstadt," he answered very calmly.

"So let me tell you about the Titans, anyway. Maybe you'll rate that a good story. The Titans were the rebels trying to restore the harmony on earth, the harmony when women ruled, and which had been destroyed by the new male hegemony. Of course they did not call themselves Titans, that was the name the winners gave to the corpses left on the battlefield. When three thousand years later the descendants of the winners christened an Atlantic liner the Titanic, they showed how little we understand our past. A ship with that name had to sink on its first voyage by the very laws—"

He cut in, in an irritated, changed, voice. "And here I always thought it had hit an iceberg. But what a learned fellow you are. Which university did you attend?"

"Why, Mr. Vinograd? Are you going to offer me a job?"

"No, I don't think so. Men like you, no matter how much you have studied, and I'm sure you have, are useless, because you have no self-discipline. The very thought of violence makes you ill because you'll always expect it to be directed *against* you. We can't even use people like you as privates in the nuclear armies. You have abolished the aristocracy but you talk non-stop about inherited rights, your own, that is ..."

Ingolstadt, forest clearing become a town, too well defended against Latin civilization, too far from the freeing seas, in the narrow streets fears and hatreds turn upon themselves, deaths by fire, rain-sodden mercenaries on two pennies a day but they are free to kill peasants by funneling the manure from the cesspools into their mouths, the way to make them tell where the gold is hidden, gentlemen on horseback chasing Jews across the cobblestoned square, killing thousands of birds with their Mannesmann shotguns, all that goes into the making of Otto Vinograd. But for the grace of God, all of us are Otto Vinograds. I had stood up without realizing it. I had not listened to Vinograd. "I know you are a famous art collector, Mr. Vinograd," I said. "Why has no one seen your collections?"

"My case in point." He sounded pleased. "For the good reason, fellow, that I do not believe in those lovefests of bringing art to the people. I'll leave that to my American colleagues with bad consciences about their Democratic Values. Do you think a French waiter understands Poussin better than I? That an Italian pizza cook needs Leonardo more than I?"

He must have rung a bell for the guard rushed in. "Toni," said Vinograd, "I'm done with this fellow. Have him fed but make absolutely sure he doesn't leave from here before me. Am I understood?"

"Yes, sir. Yes, Doctor."

58

I woke up in a silent house. The door of my room was unlocked. I wandered from basement to attic and there was nobody. I went to the Schloss and found the big front door standing open. No one there either. Not a trace of Vinograd. Someone seemed to have tried vainly to tear a zebra rug off the wall and it was badly torn with traces of what looked like dried blood. In a hallway I saw an old-fashioned telephone under a wooden cover but it was dead. In the little brick house even the coffee and the bottles of beer in the kitchen were gone. I looked outside and then I sat down on the front steps.

I heard the sound of church bells, and quite close. Eleven o'clock; it was Sunday. I decided to go to the service, I could warm myself there and maybe cadge a glass of wine afterward.

"We are guilty of mankind," the clergyman said. "We are guilty of being human beings." Was he a priest, a minister? Impossible to tell, the church and everything in it, including the man's robes, had been designed by Nuforms Associates, as it said on little notices handed out at the door.

"God was satisfied with one crucifixion, we are told," he said, "but humanity has to pay more than that. We need to give restitution, we need retribution, retribution not paid out in blood but in justice." A fine sermon, I thought. "I show you the shackles removed from a twelve or maybe ten-year-old Hottentot boy," the clergyman said. "You may read about them in the African travel diary of an Englishman whose name escapes me at the moment. It was the year of Queen Elizabeth's jubilee. We rest our case, we need no further proofs. Chardonnay '87 will be served in the rectory."

There hadn't been many people in the church but it took them a very long time to get out; whenever someone stopped to chat to a friend still sitting down, the whole column came to a halt and people appeared to wait without any impatience for the conversation to end.

Finally I was left alone in there. I badly wanted to go and drink that Chardonnay '87 or for that matter any other year the pastor cared to bring out, but I wasn't sure I could face it, what with being as disheveled as I was, a green suit which could stand up by itself from dirtiness, a stomach so empty that it made me dizzy. But where else was there to go just then, in the middle of nowhere?

I discovered I was not alone in the church after all. In front of the altar, facing a narrow table with votive candles, sat a motionless woman, her hair tied up in a red scarf. Only two candles were burning and they made the air around her shimmer. I felt or I imagined I felt a field of power emanating from there, and I hesitantly came forward. Some rows away from her I stopped and slid in. I sat down straight behind her.

She had heard me, she made a movement, but she didn't look back.

I whispered, "I am Lucas. If you are who I think—if you can tell me what to do—"

She blew out those candles and we sat still in the half-light. "You have to give us some time if you will. Please go to that reception, stay as long as you can, and then go to the brick guard house. Your help will be needed there. Will you do that?"

"They are all gone," I said. "Vinograd has gone too. And perhaps I am to blame for that. I shouldn't—"

I fell silent because she shook her head. "All will be well." She whispered too now. "Don't drink too much of her wine on an empty stomach. It's terrible stuff."

59

It was crowded around the Chardonnay. I kept myself in the background, my hands shook when I poured wine and it spilled across the table. I waited for the help, a young girl in a white apron, to pour me another glass. I could be well-nigh certain then that I had seen Maria, had exchanged a few words with her. It was a very strange idea, admittedly perhaps even an anticlimax. I looked out of the corner of my eyes at the pastor who was holding forth to a couple. *"Her* wine," Maria had said. Had I heard that right?

"That was a fine sermon, sir," the husband said, "no matter what the wife tells us." He had the little conspiratorial man-to-man smile. His wife wasn't amused.

"Why did you use the word 'proofs', Father?" she asked. "And talked about 'resting your case'? You made it sound like a court case."

"It is a court case, dear lady," the pastor said happily. "That's just what it is." He looked most unlikely from close up: maybe Nuforms had provided him too. Or her, as the case may be.

"Who is the accused then?" the husband asked.

"We are."

"And the judge?"

"There you have it. We are the accused, judge, jury, jailer, executioner. We have to put ourselves on trial, and soon, or stand condemned without trial. A predicament. But everything hangs on the outcome."

The wife nervously cleared her throat and asked, "And where is God in this allegory of yours? I assume it is an allegory? Where is He?"

"Madam, for that I refer you to the answer that the French astronomer Laplace gave, to a similar question put to him by Napoleon."

"Oh," the man and the woman both said and they smiled without asking more. Did they know? Were they afraid to find out? The reverend (if that's what he was) then asked them, "It's too warm in here, don't you agree?" and proceeded to unlock the rectory's French doors. There was such wind outside that both doors were knocked out of his hands when he turned the key, a gale blew in and started scattering the paper napkins, then the ladies' hats, and maybe in the end the reverend himself: possibly he was a devil or an angel and the wind would carry him off to the astonishment of his parishioners.

But I did not wait for that but slipped into the kitchen where the girl in the apron was watching television. "Could you help me?" I asked. "I have a very important appointment, and I had no time to shave. And no time for breakfast either."

She moved her eyes with difficulty from the screen to where I stood, and stared at me. "And?"

I tried a disarming smile. "It's for a job, you see. I need to borrow a razor, and eat something. Just bread will do." (The wine had given me the hiccups.)

"There's rolls," she said, smiling back. "I know about job interviews." She rummaged around in her handbag. "You can use my razor, if you don't mind that I use it on my legs. But shaving soap I haven't. Maybe you can use dish liquid."

That worked, sort of, although it stung nastily, and then I sat in a chair beside her, eating dry rolls and, since I had been told to stay away a long time, watching "Lifestyles." When I was back outside, the sun broke through briefly and gave me my bearings. I found my way back to the brick house, its shutters now closed and its front door locked. I circled it and then I saw Salvador. He was sitting in a little red car behind the garage.

With fear and trembling I had expected to find *her* but Salvador's face as he leaned out of the car window made it clear enough that he was alone.

Her presence changed people. Salvador whistled on his fingers, looking at me, and I slowly went over. "I'm not your dog," I said. I felt a bitter letdown now, I had waited with desperation to enter another world, a feminine world if that's not misunderstood. I was worn out by all these *men,* with their ugly faces and their pseudo-tough talk, their lack of adjectives except for "fucking." But Salvador looked far from tough. I discovered that he was sweating and very pale under his stubble. "I got hit," he told me. "You must help me, please."

"Hit?"

"I got a bullet in my arm. I can't drive any more."

"Is there no one else?"

"She said you would help me."

"But what words did she use?"

"How do you mean?" He started hunting for a cigarette in his left pocket. When he found it, he could not get his lighter to work with his left hand and I made no move to help him. In the end he threw the cigarette out of the window. "She said, 'The man is coming back here who saw me extinguish the candles. You can use that as your password.' She didn't realize I know you. You would drive me, she said."

"Going where?"

"I'll explain. But get in, get us out of here. It's dangerous, standing here."

So I got in, drove past the barbed wire, and followed the winding road away from the brick house. Salvador kept staring in the rearview mirror, but the road behind us remained empty.

60

Salvador said that "they" had driven to the narrow brick house in the night, with Maria. I didn't ask him who "they" were; I just wanted to know that we were on our way to her. I could feel his annoyance at my lack of sympathy with his adventures, but I am no longer interested in bang-bang, you're-dead history. They had come upon a scene of shouting and confusion. Some wanted to stick to the pseudo-kidnap plan and leave Vinograd unhindered, others thought the pseudo-kidnap should be turned into a real one. Maria had come to settle this but she was not forceful, for both plans were alien to her ideas. Then she had picked up the telephone, "to warn Vinograd, I think," Salvador said. At that point one of the men had produced a pistol and waved her away from the phone, an unheard-of gesture, and she had walked out of the room. "I picked up the phone, and he shot me in the arm." He had taken Maria to another place, he didn't say where, and she had asked him to go back to the brick house. "Now I can't drive any more," he ended, "my arm has gone bad."

"Are we going to her now?" I asked.

"Yes. Como no. Without doubt."

"Do you need a doctor first?"

"She—she banda—she bound my arm." He was clearly in pain and it affected his English. "First," he said, "first we must—"

Then he stopped talking and I stopped thinking about him. I thought,

I mustn't let these intrigues diminish her, diminish the shock of really meeting her. I've traveled so long. All this is just, means. The red car is just means, as once the Argo had been a means.

The car was flying and I could see out over a wide landscape as I was preparing myself. I felt I was still being tested.

After a long while I said, "You don't have to watch the rear mirror all the time. We are not being followed."

"I'm not watching the road. I'm watching him."

And then I saw that a roll of tarpaulin was stuck in the back of the car, half on the floor, half on the back seat. I turned my head to look at it, almost putting the car in a ditch. Salvador began to laugh in a very odd way. "Vinograd's in there," he said.

I frowned at him. I didn't believe it. His strange laughter embarrassed me, but the tarpaulin was indeed ridiculous. Vinograd was a force, for evil I thought, but a force; his death would have meaning, leave a tremor in the air. I would have known. Salvador lies a lot to me. Maybe for the best of reasons.

"Maria is the daughter of a French cab driver in Montreal," he suddenly said. "A man who left France in 1968, an exile like me. She was raised in a convent. The convent du Saint' Espoir. Not Saint' Esprit, Saint' Espoir. She understands every language. Yes, I will take you to her. She knows about you, Miguel told her, in Paris. About your suit too. I think he told her to make her laugh. She was sad then, in Paris."

"Did she laugh?"

"I wouldn't think. Vinograd's millions or billions. And her share which she will use to balance history. Those were her words, to balance history. But that would need a hundred years, and wealth that does not exist on this earth."

We were passing thruway signs. I looked at him. "First," he said, "we must get rid of Dr. Vinograd. He is to be taken to the shore, to the ocean. You must go east, but you can't take the Turnpike, there may be roadblocks on it."

"Why the ocean?"

"Vinograd's wife was drowned in that ocean. A murderer and his victim must be in the same body of water, and then forgiveness is achieved."

I'm leaving out Salvador's stumbling over words now, and his sudden heavy accent. That was what he said. "I don't believe all this," I answered. "Whoever or whatever is in that roll, it isn't any Dr. Vinograd."

"Okay, okay, compadre. But the roll has to go in the sea."

Darkness was closing in on us when we reached the shore road. I wound down the window of the car and could smell the ocean. We waited until it was so dark that the stars were out and dragged the tarpaulin onto the rocks. Salvador wasn't much of a help. We heaved it into the water under a rock wall, where it vas quite deep. It had been heavy, but not heavy enough.

"How did you get him rolled into that tarpaulin with one hand?" I asked when we drove on.

"My arm still worked."

"The world doesn't feel different," I said, "nothing has changed. His death would be a change."

He pulled at my arm and pointed. In the black emptiness of the little country road we were on, a brightly lit barrier had come into view, with a police car next to it.

I slowed down and drove up to it. Sticking my head out, I asked in what I assumed was a suburban voice, "What seems to be the problem, officer?"

A policeman took a step toward me with a smile, and began, "We—" as I pressed the gas down. The car jumped, knocked down the barrier, and went over it. I flew into the night.

"Bufón! Fool!" Salvador cried. "Why didn't you stop? There's no corpse in the car! What the hell!"

"Shut up!" I shouted back. "I'm sick of you. If that was a body in the car, there must be blood in the back now, mustn't there. You fucking drive if you don't like it." But we already saw the flashing red light of a police car in the mirror, and soon we heard the siren. I came to a halt under an enormous, bare oak tree.

We got out and ran around it, each of us on one side, and on into the sparse woods. We heard shouts and saw pinpoints of flashlights and then it became still. Nothing was audible but the soughing of the wind in the trees and the swish of my shoes as I picked my way across the marshy ground ready to suck me in.

61

How could a man with Vinograd's mathematical, surgical, mind get himself into a tortured plan of arranging his own fake kidnaping, a plan even poor Salvador was thinking too clever by half? How could this invulnerable man make himself vulnerable that way, since a kidnap victim in the eyes of the world is already halfway to his death?

The key to this lapse must have been Maria.

It is tricky to try and describe in factual terms Vinograd's states of mind before and after Comillas, where he had met her. Before, B.C., Vinograd had never shown the slightest chink in his armor. His chief accountant budgeted a large sum for the satisfaction of his sexual fantasies. His wife played the role he had delineated for her. When he acquired more than a million acres on the Middle Amazon, a private codicil to the sales contract specified that it would be transferred to him "emptied of natives." None of these matters would be considered by his peers as anything but normal.

After Comillas, A.C., Vinograd seemed to lose his business sense, not to say his common sense. He wanted to own Maria, but it is unclear how or for what. Buying a beautiful woman, or not succeeding in buying her (as had happened), had never bothered him in the past. Now he felt he couldn't even begin to map his strategy while his wife was still alive. Maria appeared to affect him in the precisely opposite way to Lucas; Vinograd lost his way in Comillas while Lucas found his way there, or thought he had. The human condition shows these pleasant if presumably meaningless symmetries. And Vinograd who B.C. wouldn't have dreamt of sending one dollar to a Basque independence movement, became, A.C., a benefactor who needed no further justification of a kidnap scheme than that it had brought him in contact with Maria and could continue to do so. There was a certain irony in this. It was Maria's project for indemnification of "the victims of history" which had put her in touch with the Basque movement. They trusted her and asked her to be their liaison with Vinograd. In return she received a solid chunk of Vinograd money, which set her project into motion and filled those envelopes handed out in the Bronx and at the villa miseria fair. But she thought that Vinograd was only after the promise of a tax-free headquarters in a future autonomous Basque capital, Bilbao; when she heard about the kidnap plans, all she wanted was to get out. And Miguel, who had been brought in as an alleged militant Basque, was actually a second-generation Monegasque, son of a real estate operator who had worked for the young Vinograd and had ended being pushed, or jumping, from a balcony of one of his Luxury-Prestige apartment houses.

When he was a child, Vinograd had been taken by his governess to his first motion picture. It was called *Wachsfigurenkabinet* and not precisely children's fare, but the governess of the time was Portuguese and she had dozed through it. It was the dubbed German version of an old Hollywood horror movie in which the protagonist kills the women he desires in a vat of boiling wax, in order to own them as wax statues. Vinograd's concept of owning had probably been colored by the choice of that day, unfortunately, as his governess might just as well have taken him across the street to *Lassie*. It is in the light of this, that the idea of the customs officer having saved Maria's life by his clumsy salute, becomes credible.

And its image, the harsh white and black of that salute under the border arc light, as in a World War Two newsreel—and its dark twin, the guard at the next border shaking his powerless fist—were so portentous that they became an obsession to her. Reflected in the car's mirror she had seen them as reflecting an evil past, foreshadowing a still more evil future.

She fled from Vinograd, almost literally. One afternoon she found refuge in a concert hall where her strength was restored as she was listening, almost in a trance, to the music of Albinoni. Reassured, she held on to that music and its orchestra from Chicago. She never went back to her hotel, she traveled from then on with the orchestra and was at every rehearsal and every concert. She talked to no one and no one questioned her. She did not find back the serenity of that first afternoon but she no longer felt menaced.

With a sudden clarity, in a flash, I saw myself as balancing on a dividing line between realities. I could run away from Salvador and go by myself through the night. I'd come to some solution that way, be it alone or by finding her again. If I did not do that, I would have to find my way in another reality, of police cars, Salvador's ideas of revenge, in short I'd be back in the "blood-red pattern of patriarchal history," as I've seen it described (in a book about Cassandra, by a German woman I think).

Then, before I had gone any further in my thoughts, Salvador was walking beside me again. He was out of breath, holding his wounded right arm with his left. "We have to get back to our people," he said. "I've got to get back. It'll be a disaster otherwise, they'll murder each other."

I walked on faster, he following me. There was a glimmer through the trees, a dotted line of light: it was a car passing by on a road at the end of the woods. When I got there, I started on along the asphalt.

Headlights appeared. Salvador came rushing up and posted himself in the middle of the road, waving. The car stopped. A burly man rolled down his window and asked, "Yes?"

"I was hurt," Salvador said. "Can you take us to the next town?"

"I'm not the brother's-keeper type," the man answered and started to wind up his window.

"I'll pay you!" Salvador cried.

"Fifty dollars," the man said through the crack left.

"Okay."

Salvador held the back door open for me and foolishly, fatally, I got in. We sat on the back seat together; behind us, behind a wire mesh, a German shepherd dog was standing up, constantly shifting his balance as we went through curves, his nails scraping the floor. Above the mesh, a rack held three shotguns.

Only a few miles farther we entered a village street with a few shops and a gas station, everything closed up, and dark except for the word Getty. "Here you are," the man said and stopped his car.

"This is no town," I said.

"There'll be a phone booth outside the gas station."

"This is no good to me, compadre," Salvador told him. "I'm in a great hurry."

"Let's see your fifty dollars, compadre asshole," the burly man suggested.

I looked at Salvador and he began to laugh. "I've paid out half a million dollars maybe in the past weeks," he told the man, "But I only have three dollars on me right now."

"What about you, Jack?"

I shrugged. I could see his face redden in the blueish light of the gas station sign he had stopped under. He jumped out and opened the back door. "Get out!" he screamed. "Get out, you tramps!"

I started to get out and he grabbed my arm and pulled me onto the road, so hard that I fell against him, and we staggered around like a couple of drunks. I tried to pull loose but he would not let go and got a grip on my right arm which nearly broke it. In the meantime Salvador had managed to climb into the front seat and suddenly was able to drive again. He tore off, the open doors flapping and banging, the dog in the back barking in a frenzy of rage, equalled by the rage of his master who shouted a stream of curses after his car without releasing his hold on me.

Silence suddenly, but for the whistling wind. The burly man, holding me in his jiu-jitsu grip, dragged me up the drive of the gas station where there was indeed a telephone box, and held me while he phoned the police.

63

I was going in circles that night, and I was consumed by fire. A foolish ride in this hunter's station wagon had derailed me. My fate had become absurd unless it had been Salvador's way of getting rid of me. Then at least it made sense; otherwise it was the random movement of gnats or dead leaves. In girum imus nocte et consumimur igni.

The police had arrived at the telephone box and taken us both in. They made a detour past the red car and one of the policemen asked casually, "That your car?" I said no. Two men were standing beside it, I then saw, shining flashlights.

"Were you traveling alone?" I was asked in the police station.

"Like hell he was!" the burly man cried. He was there to file his complaint.

"Who was the person this man says stole his car?"

"And my dog!"

"Just a fellow I had given a lift," I answered. "He looked all right. My car broke down and then we both hiked. I don't know his name."

"Sign here."

They were yawning as they locked me up. The burly man protested, he wanted his case tried right there and they told him to pipe down. It was more like a waiting room than a cell where they put me; thank heaven. I'd had enough cells in my life. But it was a sad place, the drabness of a discouraged little town. Insects from summers long past stuck to the walls, across from me a man was dozing who had thrown up, his vomit was in front of him on the floor and on the table. Seeing myself sit there, I thought for one desperate moment, this is simply the continuation of Frankfurt and all that came after, I never really found her. But I had. I closed my eyes and saw the shimmer of her body, her skin the color of the light filtering through the trees, it was she walking beside me in the wood and not Salvador.

The judge was holding court in a schoolhouse. On the blackboard was written my palindrome, in girum imus nocte et consumimur igni, and underneath it, eo, is, it, imus, itus, eunt. The man who had vomited was let go. Then the judge told me he'd drop my case if I would pay the burly man the fifty dollars. It was embarrassing, sensible adults fighting over such a sum.

Everyone looked at me as I started searching through the pockets of my green jacket. I guess it was clear that I knew there was nothing in there because, to the indignation of the burly man, they all laughed, even the judge.

I began to feel much better.

A clerk came in and whispered to the judge.

He turned to me. "What is your real name, sir?"

"Iberria, Your Honor."

He sighed. "Mr. Iberria, the complaint of assault is dismissed. I must order you rearrested on a federal charge of kidnap and homicide. The sergeant will read you a caution."

I heard the high voices of children behind the wall; part of the school was in use. I tried to lean against that wall to hear better, to distinguish words, because I was looking for a sign, an escape from the absurdity of my life. But they mistrusted my movement and pulled me away roughly.

64

In my cell in the federal prison of Loretto, Pennsylvania I found a book with most of the pages missing. It was a surprising find: a biography of Byron. The part left for me was the beginning, about Byron's father. If I understand it properly with so much torn out (I guess the owner used it on the toilet), this father was the black sheep of the family, packed off by his wife to France at about the time of the French Revolution, with a few pounds income and a little house in Valenciennes owned by his sister to live in. Valenciennes is in the north near the Belgian border, about where the ash-blonde in Comillas came from. It is a miserable region, I know it, never-ending rain clouds blow in from the Channel. Indeed, in the letters Byron's father sent to his sister in England there is much about the grey cold and the grey rain.

I copied one sentence from this book once the guard had let me have a notebook and a pencil, where he wrote about his "amours." He told his sister of one particular woman: "A girl at l'Aigle Rouge, an Inn here I happened there one day when it rained so hard ... She is very handsome and very tall, and I am not yet tired."

He died not long after, a suicide, it was thought.

Heaven knows there was much for me to consider at that juncture in my journey, but that one sentence written by a poor slob who had died two centuries ago, stuck in the forefront of my thoughts. It haunted me.

I saw that inn, "one day when it rained so hard," he alone, lonely, wandering down the streets of somber Valenciennes that turned its face away, taking shelter from the rain in the inn, the two of them in the empty taproom, he on a heavy wooden chair, looking at her who is standing in the kitchen entrance with her eyes on the open door and the water running down in streams from the ledge and the glistening leaves of the tree in front. An afternoon when time did not move, when sighs hovered endlessly in the air. The consolation found in their embrace, the girl flipping up her skirt and allowing him to come down between her long legs.

I did not feel sorry for him nor for her, to the contrary. I thought that the few moments such as those had been, were perhaps all there was in one lifetime, indeed all that there is for the justification of the vast structure of human life on earth. I mean, I felt that everything, from when people invented the wheel and then built stone houses and towns and inns, and invented nationalities—if that whole fabric had yielded up just that little encapsuled happiness or nostalgia for those two making love in an attic of the inn on an old eiderdown, an oil lamp, whispering, and the rain hammering on the roof, it justified all, it was enough to fulfill our happiness and our sadness—as he had known, perhaps, when he killed himself.

But it was a mistaken idea then (a snare and a delusion as we used to say as children, words taken from one of our favorite night-time stories), our asking, "More!", our talking of happiness *pursued,* wrongs righted, compensation, restitution.

If those few moments are all, if a low wave of nostalgia is all we share with the universe (all the goodwill the universe has to show us), then my journey has not been a destined search but a getting lost by myself in a maze built by myself. Then I made up that Convent du Saint' Espoir. Hope of what? What right do we have to ask more of life than our rainy afternoon in the Inn of the Red Eagle?

65

In a courtroom of black and white shadows Lucas was sometimes leaning on the table, sometimes sitting up straight. Sitting up straight was better, he had been told by his defense lawyer, an old and very unprepossessing person but the only willing one they had been able to find for him.

The lawyer spoke almost inaudibly and when he said, "objection" or asked what he perhaps thought of as a penetrating question, only Lucas could hear him. The prosecutor, the judge, and the jury quickly became used to this and went on with the case as if they were among themselves.

They had begun to act as if they were rehearsing a trial for television, or possibly the judge, once a law professor at the state university, was thinking of the mock trials he used to run as an exercise for his graduate students. When he adjourned the court, he said, "That's it for today, I hope to see you all here tomorrow," and always with a little joke that he knew he was competing with the baseball or football season. And Lucas cringed when his lawyer turned directly to him, for the man exhaled the sour smell of a thousand horrible meals, cooked by a wife who hated him, and left undigested while he shuffled his useless briefs.

The Vinograd empire had handed out instructions to stymie any moves undertaken on Lucas' behalf, for it certainly did not want "interesting developments." It just wanted it all to be over. In a turnabout operation (which had caused laughter during the lunches of its local public relations people), it had spent heavily on non-publicity, and this with success. Yes, the victim had been rich and powerful but he had been a man shrinking from public attention in life as in death; the murderer, an unhinged amateur, had acted blindly, *the way a toppling tree kills a man blindly,* and his story was bare of human interest. He was a bum as the almost amusing testimonies of an American Express witness and an officer of Lucas' bank showed when they produced various bills paid with an invalid credit card and checks cashed abroad without funds to cover them. Thus the occasional report on an inside page of *The Inquirer* should really be all that was warranted, and early on the judge had been generously rewarded for not allowing any television within a thousand feet of the courtroom—a ruling much admired as heralding a new age in media restraint. The ruling had been annoying, though, when a truck had amputated a child's leg just within the thousand-feet limit; the TV crew wanting to record the boy's dying words had had to drag him out of the forbidden circle first.

Lucas looked through the dirty windows for signs of spring, birds, blue sky, he stared at the dandruff on his lawyer's shoulders.

He waited for the courtroom doors to open and for Maria to enter.

Finally he withdrew within a solipsistic circle.

His fingerprints were found on the door of the brick house as on the steering wheel of the little red car and in the Schloss where Vinograd was last seen. Fibres or bits of tarpaulin were in the garage, in the back of the car, and on the rocks at the ocean shore near where the car was found. Or would have been on those rocks if the tides had not washed them away, a hiatus rectified by a police expert.

The doorman of the Philadelphia golf club where Vinograd had been playing recognized Lucas as someone who had been hanging around outside the clubhouse. A homeless tramp, picked up when he tried to change a thousand-dollar bill, identified Lucas as the man who had given him the money. The bill was traced back to one of the ransom payments.

Claire appeared as the only witness summoned by the defense, and several jury members sighed at the wistful smile she had for Lucas when she sat down. She looked very smart. But all that Lucas's mumbling lawyer could get from her was her opinion that Lucas was gentle, "too gentle for his own good" (laughter in the courtroom). The prosecutor managed to make her admit that Lucas was a loser.

Thus, he was found guilty.

66

But away from the courtroom odd things happened that winter. "New Voices Are Heard," as a New York Times editorial put it, and those voices were plants sprouting from Maria's seed money, her share in what was left of the ransom.

In the province of Choco, Colombia, a group of peasants who had mysteriously become peso millionaires, wrecked a cocaine factory and plowed under twelve hundred acres of coca.

In Bangkok one evening, some thirty child prostitutes castrated their customers of the moment all at the same time, or at least had a good try with scissors, Swiss Army knives, and eyebrow tweezers. Then they fled together on an Air India plane chartered anonymously, bringing the local sex-tourist industry to a bloody ending.

Here in the U.S., the black super of the town hall of Savannah, Georgia, filed suit for damages on behalf of his great-grandfather against the family that had owned the man; and after being addressed by one of the most famous (and most expensive) lawyers in the country, the jury awarded him the great-grandfather's original purchase price of eight hundred dollars plus compound interest at five percent per annum since January 1, 1863. In *Hopi vs. People* a fancy Los Angeles lawyer submitted, on the basis of an obscure treaty clause, a claim of the Hopi nation to a ten dollar visitor's tax from every resident of Arizona, including women and children.

When that last case became widely known, a welter of lawsuits followed. New York lawyers in corporate jets, British lawyers in chauffeured limousines, and their French, Irish, and even Russian confrères appeared with calfskin briefcases full of impeccable documents and began filing suits on behalf of Irishmen, Poles, Jews, Indians, and black Americans. Law courts everywhere had to empty out closets and even waiting rooms to find space for all the papers arriving.

But equally sudden and without people knowing why, it was all over. The elegant lawyers returned to their corporate takeovers and divorces, Bangkok sent out scouts to buy new children, the Hopis accepted a failing shopping center in full settlement of their claim, and the millionaire Colombian peasants disappeared from this earth. What had happened was that Maria's funds had run out.

However: it was seen that state capital archives and libraries did not return to their former quiet. To the nervousness of librarians and civil servants, lines formed at their doors before opening time, lines of aging hippies with knapsacks, American Indians, retired miners, orthodox Polish Jews, and even an Eskimo here and there. These people then spent hours scanning books and documents without asking for any assistance, without chatting, without coffee breaks. They were preparing something but it wasn't clear what. The FBI was warned and local police executed some random arrests for the hell of it, but the only case they made stick was against a man who had dropped his burning cigar stump in a library paper basket as he came in.

67

The lawyer came to see me and said, "I wouldn't appeal if I were you. You'll save a hell of a lot of money."

"I thought you were appointed by the court."

"True, true—" His voice was becoming inaudible again. "Brr shh brr trr trr what I mean, if I don't have to continue with your case, I can take the postal workers arbitration. That's a lot more fruitful."

"Fruitful?"

"The money tree." He laughed, the first time I heard him do so. It sounded awful.

"Let me get this straight, are you saying you'll make more money?" I asked.

"Right. Right. This case is poison, take it from me."

I walked over to the barred window of the lawyers' room as they called it. I could see a row of pine trees, and a bit of road. A trailer-truck rolled by; it was so far off that you could not hear a sound. I told myself, I have to pay attention.

"I'll make it up to you if you don't appeal," lawyer Dandruff said. "I'll give you a split from my fee, a couple of hundreds at least. Maybe a grand."

"What good is that to me if they execute me?"

"They won't. They never do—and if worse comes to worst, you can give me the name of your favorite charity. That will be a nice gesture, for the media."

"I thought one had to appeal, with a death penalty."

"There are always ways," he muttered. Muttering he was much clearer than talking.

"Please leave," I said.

"Okay, okay. No need to take offense."

"And go see a dentist." I called out after him.

"Hey man," the guard told me, "Never pick a fight with your lawyer. He's your best friend. In very bad cases your absolutely last friend."

I laughed, he appreciated that.

When that same guard brought me my dinner, a plate of pasta and coffee, he asked, "I hope you like coffee? Well, bottoms up as they say."

Under the metal mug a piece of paper had been stuck which read, *Apply for visit of your half-sister Maria, let them call 212-831-7744.*

Only people whose visit I requested could come and see me.

The message undid me. I had accepted that my mind was in a disordered state, accepted that my wandering, with little money for food and no one to speak to, had led me into a fantasy existence. The existence of an imaginary and solitary Jason. Without shipmates.

I had been unnerved by the vision of a woman seen from a distance and I had not seen her again.

Three thousand years of corruptive history were as unmovable as a mountain.

I had spent the months in my cell learning these conclusions by heart.

Now a piece of paper was brought to me, telling me that she did exist, that there was a link between us. She would come and visit me, enter this filthy prison, if only I made the necessary request. I fell into panic. I did not dare see her but I knew it was also inconceivable not to see her.

I had never been in the visitors' room. They took me there three or four days later (I could not keep track) and I found comfort in the discoloring of the wire glass separating us from the visitors. I did not wish to be seen clearly. I feared both seeing and being seen. I had been severed from both, irreparably I had thought.

I sat down where they told me to and waited. The room was empty. The guard, a pale, tired, man, went to sit in a corner on a little wooden platform. He took a long time adjusting the angle of his chair according to some unknown rule or criterion.

She entered even more hidden in her scarf than the morning in the Nuforms church. She sat down across from me behind the wireglass and I saw it was not her, but Claire.

Now my circle was broken with violence, as of the soldier who broke Archimedes' circle and then killed him. From the night of the burly man trying to break my arm to that moment, I had been freed from my body, looking down at it from great height, and with no emotions to experience except at times in the dead of night with the rain hammering on the roof of the Valenciennes inn.

I tried to greet Claire. "Why did you call yourself Maria?" I asked and she said something about her job and embarrassment. I saw that she considered it brave of herself to have come and I guessed that only by keeping a taxi waiting had she managed to enter the building. She asked me how I was, and I answered that she shouldn't stay too long, with her taxi. She blushed but I had not meant it that way; who could blame her? I don't know what she said after that nor what I answered.

I was lucky enough to stumble down the iron staircase on the way back to my cell and lose consciousness, anew.

When I came to, I was on a camp bed in a little white and green room. It was early morning or early evening, a hesitant, double light shone in. The only sound was the ticking of a big old-fashioned alarm clock such as I had during my school days. I used to wrap that clock loosely in an old shirt or the ticking would have kept me awake. “You must wrap it,” I said to a nurse who sat on a chair near my bed and we looked at one another.

This woman had her hair in a scarf too, and when she saw my eyes open, she undid the scarf and shook her hair free in a mysteriously fierce movement. She was Maria, she whom I call Maria.

All I could think of saying was, “I never expected to be in jail so many times in my life,” and then I closed my eyes again.

“We are not doing so badly, you and I,” she told me. “Look at me. Come, look at me.”

“In a moment.” For I was afraid, afraid of the deadly disappointment, of the emptiness that would follow seeing her face. Thus a mystic for the very same reason must be afraid to set his eyes on God. How could a dreamed recognition survive the anticlimax of a physical presence?

But when I finally forced myself to look at her, at the narrow face set free from the silk scarf, there was no shock of normalcy and I was suddenly and totally at peace again, as I had been once in the dark street in Comillas, with the stone saint shining in the moonlight.

My vision became clearer and I saw that she was wearing a denim uniform which seemed to be nowhere in contact with her body as if it were a diver's or space suit.

"Yes, I am in jail too," she said. "That's why it took so much time. But it's my last day. All will be well. All will be well!"

"The judge has condemned me to death by injection."

She violently shook her head. "All will be well. Don't be afraid."

I wasn't. I imagine that when my tree killed the border guard, I forfeited the right to be afraid anyway.

"We must start all over," she said. She was speaking so softly that I could hardly hear her. "There is a new Vinograd, his brother."

"Oh—" I could not think of anything else to say.

"He has changed his first name to Otto, in honor of his murdered brother, that's what they say in the paper."

I shook my head. "It's him, it's the same man!" I tried to shout but my voice was too croaky. "I knew it, I knew Salvador was lying, that carpet was too light."

"I know," she said. "But we can never prove it. His fingerprints, his blood, they're all different, they showed affidavits on the news."

My thoughts became crystal clear. "Come closer, Maria," I whispered. "I must tell you about works of art. They are hidden in caves and they are the way for you to get money and save your work, the paintings and statues and tapestry of the world. I don't know how much of it, who knows, perhaps the lot, and the incunabula, and everything, were stolen or bought and they are stored in caves near the Gannett Peak in the Rocky Mountains. The people who live in the foothills there must be aware of something. And if you fly over those hills, it would be impossible not to feel them when you are near. If you can get hold of only some …" I had to pause.

She nodded. "We will find them," she whispered. "And we will free you." She put her hand on my forehead. But an orderly I had not even noticed, shouted furiously, "No touching the prisoners! Take it away! Take it away!"

I stared at him. He was not shouting at her, she was no longer there, he was shouting at another prisoner who was carrying a basin with blood and vomit. "Take it away," he said again less loudly. And then, looking at me, "You'll be all right now," and he wiped my face and the dirty sheet with a paper napkin, not unkindly. "Go back to sleep, man."

69

It came to pass in those days that there was an election for the governorship of the state.

The campaign revolved around the one issue of crime. "In the single year 1600," an early television commercial for one of the candidates said, "England hanged a thousand criminals. There were four million Englishmen at the time. By cutting away the rotten wood they were on their way to become the greatest empire the world had seen. Then they turned soft, and they descended to being a second-rate nation." At a press conference the candidate was asked if it meant that he wanted fifty thousand people a year executed in the United States. "We do that already," he answered with a flashing smile, "with our automobiles. I would like us to be more selective." The media agreed that the man was crazy but his ratings in the polls went up.

He then explained that his answer had been flippant. "I am suggesting maybe one tenth of that number. No one *has* to murder a fellow American. But if they do, if they dislike us that much, we have the right to invite them to leave us—quickly, through the exit door of the gas chamber." His fans put, "Love Us or You'll Leave Us" bumper stickers on their cars.

The death penalty now became not only a political but also a fashionable subject. The Sunday sections of the papers compared the possible methods of execution in detail, with drawings and medical charts. Conservative religious lobbies questioned the so-called humanitarian swift death. A slower death would give a criminal time to repent, saving his or her soul. "NO to the easy way out," became their slogan.

A Texan toy manufacturer created execution kits complete with the gurney on which the criminal is strapped there, a miniature last meal, doctor, prison governor, TV crew, poison needle. A New York toy firm overcame the handicap of states without death penalty by producing a Victorian-England kit (they called it "the Sherlock Holmes Execution Kit") with gallows, rope, hangman, and little black flag.

Lucas' friendly guard had been transferred and his successor fed Lucas the newspaper stories about these developments, perhaps naively rather than sadistically for he always added, "You've nothing to worry about, the guy who's in now will win and he pardons everyone." Lucas tore out the picture of the gurney which is really a stretcher on wheels. He had to look at it closely. The concept of walking into a room with a number of officials and then *lie down* in order to be killed was impossible for him to fathom. It led him back to the terror he had felt on crossing the Paris square, Place de l'Hôtel de Ville, once Place de Grèves, although he could not know why.

This death penalty craze (to use the phrase from one of our more expensive fashion magazines) ended abruptly when a deranged ex-convict shot and killed the candidate in question, at what had been billed as a Crime with Punishment Rally. In its wake, the sitting governor was urged by his campaign advisors to announce that he had come back from his policy of automatic pardons for prisoners on death row. The polls were bearing out this advice. The governor did what they asked, fittingly at a memorial service for his assassinated opponent.

70

Vast caves had been widened farther into a series of cellars, two thousand feet inside the lower slope of the Gannett Peak of the Rocky Mountains, at the end of a dirt road from Lenore. The mountain is in that section of the range which is popular with oil and real estate millionaires from the East Coast for their atomic-war family retreats, just as for no known reason of fashion Sunbelt and Texan millionaires and billionaires built theirs farther north, between Bozeman and the Canadian border. It will be interesting for anyone still around to see which was the wisest choice.

In these cellars, "RM Gannett Cave 1 & 2" on the Vinograd labels, behind a steel door as of a safe deposit room, "Jerusalem Liberated" hung with Goya's "Dos de Mayo" and Poussin's "Et in Arcadia Ego." Hung, because Vinograd's expert had told him that the paintings should not stay crated but hang in the temperature-steady air. After all, the expert said, he could not be expected to estimate the time they would have to stay in there. Perhaps for as long as the mountain would exist. This way they would last better.

As no one set foot there, no effort was made to hang them in any historical, museum, order. Of course not. It was simply a matter of size. A copy of Rembrandt's Hundred Guilder Print just fitted in between two small Vermeers, one above it, one below. A Zadkine iron martyr stood in a corner with his face to the wall, his fist not reaching for the sky but leaning against the rock, and so on. A tapestry commissioned by Louis the Fourteenth from a landscape by Jan van Goyen hung partly folded over a box of antique rifles, the selfsame ones with which Louis' general Pichegru had had the Inhabitants of the Dutch rivertown Vechten (twice painted by Van Goyen) fusilladed in the winter of 1672 because one of them had wounded a French soldier in the head with a stone. The rifles are finely worked. (Two, probably belonging to officers, have been engraved with almost medieval patience, yet it could be said that modern warfare started with the fusillade at Vechten.) And right next to the box as if part of one and the same tableau mourant, sat a cigar-smoking man cut by an American sculptor out of the same stone which was now surrounding him.

It is tempting to assume as Lucas had done, though perhaps a romantic fiction, that such a concentration of artists' work of centuries in one place must cause a vibration, a notable charge, the way a source of running water does in a divining rod. While the rifles of Pichegru are but wood and metal, a Van Goyen is but wood and linen, couldn't the emotions of their creators still react? Could creativity itself not be measurable in such concentration? And if nothing else, all those vehicles bringing in this stuff over many months must have been noticed, even though old and battered GMC trucks had been used to make the transports less conspicuous. The truckers were paid standard haulage charges; anything more might only have made them suspicious. Not that they'd have given a damn. A hundredweight is a hundredweight and a mile is a mile.

It would be proper (in the sense Lucas gives to the word) if all this could be stolen back, or better, taken back. Sold back to its places of origin and reappearing in our lives, it would provide the money for those expiatory payments of Maria's enterprise. Ransoming our own past. There is a painful appropriateness to it, our best paying for our worst.

Therein lies a good reason for doubt too. Such symbolism is too good to be true, surely.

71

I saw her one more time in the prison hospital.

It was less simple, that second time. So many thoughts had been wandering through my head in the days between, thoughts that came and vanished like birds flying across a winter sky. That sounds a bit too flowery but it fits so well: my mind was really empty and grey. The time that I recognized myself as a modern-day hero, a modern-day Jason, heaven help me, seemed far away.

It was twilight in the hospital room. The sky had suddenly darkened, a storm was brewing. They hadn't turned on the light, maybe because it was only two in the afternoon. They have rules about those things. In the Boston of my youth I once sat a whole desperate Sunday on a bench of the Aquarium, in the half-light filtered through the green water. It was that kind of light that filled the hospital. She came to me under the surface of the ocean of forgiveness, as they had called it for Vinograd and his murdered wife.

I looked at her eyes, not at the her who was saying words I could not hear, but through her eyes into herself. If I willed it strongly enough, I could transfer myself over in her and survive that way. For in those moments I was certain that she was indeed like a goddess, the Greek goddess from the lake of Nemi, that she was outside my time and born long before there was a town called Montreal with taxis driving around in it.

She put a hand on my forehead but took it away when I shook my head. “It’s forbidden,” I said. What else to say? “You look like a lady in distress out of Don Quichote. Like that morning in the church with the mad clergyman.”

She laughed, a soft laugh. “But the mad clergyman was a woman. Think of what she said! But you must have realized.”

“Yes. Yes I do now.”

“I will read you something from a book I brought you,” she said, “because they told me I am not allowed to leave it with you.”

“It is too dark to read here,” I answered but she shook her head. “Listen. ‘Hair began growing from antelope skin gloves, woollen blankets were unraveling and turning into the fleeces of sheep in distant pastures. Cupboards, cabinets, beds, crucifixes, tables and blinds disappeared into the darkness in search of their ancient roots beneath forest trees. Armor—’”

“Armor,” I broke in, “iron works, keys, copper cooking pots, were melting and forming a swelling river of metal running into the earth through roofless channels.”

“Hey you fellow, shut up,” someone said.

It was now totally dark in there.

And yet she restored me, I am restored to my road.

72

When attorney Vinetti, State Representative Plimsol, and Salvador carrying the money, were admitted to the state governor's office, they saw they were in trouble. The governor was not alone. He had a dapper grey-haired man with him whom he introduced as his personal counsel.

"We hoped for a private interview, Governor," Vinetti said.

"Anything you want to say to me, you may say in front of my friend and advisor here."

"Right. Governor, it's like this, a prominent citizen who wants to remain anonymous for the moment, is planning a donation to the Boys Home of your wife, I mean the one your wife is chairperson of. A fine donation, a hundred thousand dollars. We read that you and she will go there for the yearly dinner with the boys, and it seems a fine occasion to present the check, to get the home some, eh, fine publicity."

The governor did not look impressed. "Yes, that would be fine," he said. "Of course Rita will be grateful. Let me take you to her private secretary, to Jim, and then you can make all the arrangements in peace."

"Ah yes, that is a fine idea," Vinetti said. "But we are making some other calls this morning, perhaps it will be better if we make an appointment with this Jim by telephone."

"Shit," Plimsol said when they were standing in front of the state house once more. "He was scared, he thought it was entrapment."

"He doesn't need our hundred thousand dollars. Vinograd's men have been through here before us. You can tell."

Judge Jones did receive them in his chambers alone.

"Is your name really Jones, Your Honor?" Salvador asked.

"I beg your pardon. What do you mean, sir?"

"Oh well, you know, like when a man signs in at a hotel with a girl, he'll put down Mr. and Mrs. Jones, ha ha, no offense of course, Your Honor."

"Don't mind him, Your Honor," Vinetti said. "Hispanics have a very lively sense of humor."

"So it would seem," Judge Jones said. "But to get to business, gentlemen. You want a retrial for, for—" He went down the list on his desk with a stumpy pencil. "For Arturo Panavetti who burned down the house of his ex-wife."

"No, no, Your Honor. For Lucas. I mean for John Lucas. That's to say, John Iberria."

"Well, who is it to be?"

"Iberria. Definitely Iberria."

The judge stared at his list. "Right. Here he is. Now you say you realize the burden on the taxpayer, our overcrowded court calendar, and the—"

"Absolutely, Your Honor, say no more. Here is the briefcase. Salvador. Fifty thousand dollars in twenties and fifties."

"Those are good cigars on that desk, gentlemen. You may want a smoke while I count this. Unless you're a bunch of health freaks of course, ha ha."

"I don't quite trust that man," Plimsol told them when they were outside. "He doesn't look, you know, he doesn't look—"

"Juridical," Vinetti suggested.

"Judicial."

"Let's go to the prison," Vinetti said. "There's no point in all these shortcuts, it has to be done the hard way. Right, Salvador, your people want it that way? We have to start from the prison governor on down again, and not skip a single guard, cleaning woman, typist. It's a drag but we might as well do it now. Better safe than sorry."

"I don't trust the prison governor either," Plimsol muttered. "Five hundred dollars, who ever heard of that. It's too cheap if you know what I mean."

Salvador shrugged. "Iberria was supposed to be taking the rap, as you call it in this ff, eh, in this fine country. If it comes to that, so be it then. We will have done our best."

73

And yet, in the race against time I fell, and was caught. Two guards came to my cell door and told me to get my things together—it took three minutes—and then walked me through corridors I had not seen before, across courtyards, past a line of abandoned urinals where water dripped down the stained porcelain, over bare ground where nothing grew or moved, through a cemetery of woods where crosses, made from slats of packing crates, had been planted, some with numbers, some with words, "Florida," "Produce Of," and back in through a low iron door.

We came to a row of cages as of an old-fashioned animal park, brightly lit by wire-protected ceiling lamps. In each, a man was standing or pacing like a bear or a tiger. One stuck out an arm between the bars and tried to grab my jacket. The guard struck at his hand with his nightstick but he missed and I heard a weak laughter behind us.

"What is this place?" I asked but I knew.

At the last turn we had passed a guardroom facing a metal mirror reaching from floor to ceiling, enabling the man on duty to look in two directions at once. And as I passed this mirror with a guard on each side of me, I had recognized myself as the man in the television photograph on Miguel's desk in the Salle Martel.

The guards looked annoyed. My question had annoyed them.

"Never mind," I said.

"It's death row, Mac," one of the guards told me.

"Not to worry," the other added. "Most of our guests here live to a ripe old age."

They took away the two paper bags with my possessions, for these had increased already to where they filled two bags. "Just a routine check," they said. "It'll all get back to you." Then they waited until I had sat down on my bunk and closed my door carefully, although the clanging of iron on iron vibrated for a long time afterward.

"I won't be able to sleep, not with that light right above my head," I said to them as they stood next to each other outside, eyeing me.

"People get used to most anything."

From that morning on I was watched. They were not afraid of me but afraid for me. They were afraid I would try to cheat the gallows as it was once called, when men and women, and children, were hanged in front of their fellow beings.

Under that perpetual ceiling light, like an upended open war grave with its perpetual flame, I began my waking dream of standing in a waiting line.

I tried to starve my body, now my last enemy, but had to go on feeding it uselessly and wastefully. Feeding it and emptying its waste in the gurgling, seatless toilet in the corner of my cell, with the guards making a point of looking away. I refused to wash or shave it, although they kept asking me to. Such euphemistic acts were beyond me: my body was brought here to be stopped from being.

74

But on a soundless morning after I had walked my twenty minutes round and round a courtyard under a leaden sky, I found a different guard waiting at my cell door. "Iberria, neaten yourself up. Lawyer here to see you," he said. We followed long, molded, walls again, and iron corridors. We crossed on a plank indifferently thrown over a construction pit full of black water and like an oubliette. I began to be afraid. "Where are we going?" I asked him.

He tried to unlock a door. "Death-row lawyers room," he said, studying his keys. "Here you go." A room with a table and two chairs, a little barred window, a dangling light bulb. A stopped wall clock and a calendar for the year 1963. "Just sit and wait," he told me. There was an oddity about his behavior, it was without the mixture of authority and pity they used here as a rule.

I sat at the table. Irritation now rather than fearfulness: irritation at the idiocy of the human condition forcing us to think too little of others' lives and too much of our own. Very much later I heard him try all those keys of his once more before the door opened and closed.

"The man behind the candle," she said. "Please look up."

I had known it would be her but I had also known, within that same thought, that if I admitted the knowledge to myself, the truth of it would be shattered.

I did look up. She was wrapped in an enormous woollen overcoat and she carried a briefcase and wore a hat. She was disguised as a lawyer, a dreamt lawyer, but this time she was not a dream. And now finally I understood her beauty. It was not, of course not, beauty as an object for others. It was a manifestation of harmony, clumsy words for what was so simple.

"And how do I look?" I asked inanely. "They gave me leave to wear my own green suit, for my last—" I stopped myself.

In the silence, the old dead clock started ticking again.

"It is a very good suit," she said gravely.

"It is. It was my armor almost."

Now my body no longer felt moribund. Nothing was lost yet, not even that first battle I have talked about so much.

"We are starting again, from the beginning," she said. "From the very beginning because Vinograd got most of the money back. But never mind, for we found the caves! Vinograd's caves!"

"Hurrah," I muttered.

"It was so easy. At times even we are lucky. A painting, not bigger than this"—she waited until I finally opened my eyes again and looked at her hands—"one of the most perfect things ever created, by a man called Chardin, was hanging in a gas station there, right above the cash register. Salvador saw it. The gas station man had found it in the road, miraculously, an authentic omen, that painting falling off, breaking out of its box. You are no longer a man in despair. Your fate has become my responsibility. Don't shake your head. It is not by my choice, nothing in our history is by choice. I have since realized that I was aware of you in Comillas, that I stared at you through Vinograd's smokescreen."

I now had the courage to smile at her. "Please," I said. "I have never thought of you, looked at you, except in the way a mortal looked up at Artemis, at the goddess." "Or as the cat looked at the king," I added, for I feared that I had sounded ridiculous.

But she pursued her own thoughts. "My idea is not conceivable. I know that. The upending of history is not conceivable. Never mind! Neither is the day when our sun rises so weakened that only the lichen will survive until evening, and that day will come too. And the private day for each man and woman when the universe disappears forever. We can only try. Try to have more days of harmony at the end than of cruelty at the beginning."

She had talked so fast that she was out of breath. She waited.

My heart seemed to have stopped beating.

"I do not know you," I whispered. I tried to raise my voice. "I don't know your name. I don't know who you are, the Greek goddess of my imagination or the daughter of the cabdriver in Montreal. I do not even know any more if you are sitting there, across this table from me. It isn't fair."

I sounded like a child with those last words, but such considerations didn't matter to me anymore.

"It's fair because I don't know myself," she said very slowly now. "Perhaps, almost certainly, we are meant to be what we are recognized to be. If you see me as—I often see a lake in my dreams, and a sacred tree—"

She fell silent.

She was such that nothing she said could be derided. As for me, a person condemned to death has at least this, he can no longer be ridiculous.

She seemed to study me with great care, to weigh me in a balance.

Then in a wave of happiness I came to believe that she, Montreal cabdriver's daughter, would be an Artemis of our time, the goddess who was called Diana of the Crossroads in Latin. No one with less power would dream of resisting the iron in our age. But, clearly, I didn't measure up to such a fight. Throughout my journey I had thought there has to be a new kind of heroism in this world, the very opposite of that heroism of the male world that started with Achilles, the heroism of anger. And so there must be. But I hadn't quite measured up. I was not a new hero, a hero for our time. It would only be just if she was; it would start with a woman.

I had had a long search for her, with many prisons, with blood, and with Two Buildings as in that fairy tale. I was now in my Third Building. I had almost made it, but only almost. Yet I was happy.

The light bulb flickered and then went out. I looked at her in the drab diffusion of daylight that entered through the barred window.

"Whoever you are—" I began. And went on quickly, muttering more than speaking, "I did try to find you, but not with any pretence that I measured up to—I am too weak for you. I am too weak. I am, well, I am *not* many things. At the end of this bloody century you—you gave me back a sense of hope, of security. It sounds odd, saying that here. What you made me feel is, perhaps there will be justice at the end of the day. And as for my ending up here, believe it or not, I don't think I mind much. My life has been a screw-up. This journey was the good thing in it. So let me play out my heroic scene."

"But you are wrong," she said solemnly. "For it is your Chardin! When the light went out just now, in fact all the power is off, you did that, for it went off for the simple and natural reason that it was the Chardin money that bribed the electrician at the main power switch. Did you forget that we are going to do away with heroics?"

"Doing away with heroics—" I repeated.

"We are going to escape from here," she said calmly. And she wrapped her enormous coat around us both.

The calendar fell down, the walls began to crack.

*

MYSTERIOUS PRISON BREAK IN PENNSYLVANIA
Philadelphia, Feb 19 — State authorities in Pennsylvania failed so far to account for yesterday's prison break at the Loretto Correctional Institute which started with a power failure and a mud slide destroyed the east wall, and at the precise time that the prison governor and his senior staff, complaining of nausea after a Rotarian luncheon, had left their offices …

*

Latonia antique ut solita es bona hospites gentem:
Diana, daughter of Leto, as of old safeguard your people!